INCUBUS
KISS

INCUBUS
KISS

ROBIN THORN

DEATH KISS BOOK ONE

HER

PROLOGUE

I paced along the dark street of Briarwood, pools of misted lamplight mapping out my path towards the rundown bar. I could hear my quick breaths, my footsteps tapping out a rhythm on the pavement. The street was quiet, abandoned, just a truck-stop off the highway. Nothing seemed out of the ordinary or exceptional. At least, not from the outside.

I was close now. The thrum of bass music seeping from the brick walls.

Just a little further.

I ran the last few steps and pulled open the door. The rush of opium scents hit the back of my throat, intoxicating me.

Alone, I moved numbly through the crowded bar. It was dark, smoky, and I could feel dozens of sets of eyes on me, tearing me apart with their hungry gazes.

I shouldn't have come here. Already dread was seeping into my consciousness. I should never have ended up in a place like this, but now that it I'd started, I couldn't stop. My body screamed for more.

For *Him*.

I caught sight of *him* now, through the smoky haze and the hive of bodies moving around me, dressed in tight clothes and black leather.

His golden eyes pierced the crowd, somehow landing only on me in the darkened bar. Somehow needing me just as much as I needed him.

Or maybe that was wishful thinking.

My heart rate quickened as I approached the cordoned off area of the bar, where two burly security guys guarded a red rope that marked the VIP area.

Please let me through I willed. I glanced down at my outfit, a skin-tight leather mini, just like he always liked. My long black hair tumbled loosely over my shoulders and my fingernails

painted blood red.

I urged him silently. *Please tell them to let me in.*

I'd been here just a few nights earlier, and I'd only just managed to get access inside VIP. Maybe the security guards would recognise me tonight though. Perhaps they'd let me in if they knew I was with *Him*.

Unless he didn't want me tonight, the harrowing thought suddenly occurred to me. Maybe he was waiting for someone else. Maybe he was bored of me.

I trailed my fingers over my leather skirt, a second skin to me now. The hairs on my arms stood on end in the chill of the room.

Please choose me.

The security guard glanced me up and down with his crimson stare, then slowly craned his neck towards the private room. His focus went to the dark-haired man in the shadowed booth—the man with the golden eyes.

To my relief, the man responded with an almost imperceptible nod.

My stomach flipped as the security guard drew back the red rope, granting me access.

I stumbled over myself as I almost ran to him. Another guy was sitting beside him in the booth, and the stranger shook his head with a sigh at the sight of my arrival. With a grim expression, he rose to his feet and stepped out from the booth, allowing room for me.

"Goodbye, Sam," *He* murmured as the other left the table.

"Go easy on her, Leonard," Sam replied, and he walked back towards the main bar.

But I barely registered anything.

Leonard. His name was soft as honey. As sharp as thorns.

I slid into the booth beside Leonard, and at once his mouth moved closer to mine. My lips parted as he breathed me in. My blood rushed through my body, causing my head to spin.

A trickle of black smoke leaked from my mouth. I trembled in ecstasy.

He should stop now, I thought vaguely. *He usually stops now.*

But he drew in another breath.

And another.

Then another, until there was no more left for him to take.

CHAPTER ONE

It was the breath that woke me. The hot brush of air that moved over my face, dragging me from the pits of sleep. I knew it wasn't the right time to wake. My body was still heavy with sleep; my eyelids crusted together. Pressure weighed my body down, pinning me to my bed.

Stefan. My name, a broken whisper that stirred my consciousness. I opened my eyes, and I half expected someone to be standing over me. I was wrong. The dark of my room welcomed me.

A shuffling noise sounded from the corner of my room.

My entire body chilled. I wasn't alone.

I sat up and flipped the lamp on, flooding my dorm room in a too-bright ochre glow.

"Who's there?" I choked.

It took a moment for my eyes to adjust as my focus moved quickly around the room, darting over in the pine wardrobe and desk that filled the small space. And then my eyes landed on *Her.* A girl was stood in the corner of my room, motionless. She was tall, willowy, with a curtain of long black hair. At once, my fear dissolved into anger. Hazing had ended over a month ago, how dare someone come into my room in the middle of the night!

"What do you think you're playing at?" I shouted, my voice cracking.

She didn't respond.

I'd only been living on campus since September, and it was closing in on mid-December now. It was possible that I didn't know every live-in student in Dorm Block D, but I was almost sure I'd never seen her before.

A whisper of night air blew in from the open window across the room. The winter chill crept in, holding me in its icy vice.

Funny, I didn't remember leaving the window open.

All a sudden, my vision started to blur. It was as though I couldn't focus on her anymore. Almost as though she wouldn't allow me to. Her sinuous raven hair turned into ripples in my distorted vision, like thick black smoke, as insubstantial as she was. The bedside lamp flickered, and the bulb gave way with a pop.

My room was void of light. I couldn't see her anymore.

"Who are you?" I rasped. As I spoke, my breath escaped in a cloud of mist.

Shaking, I fumbled blindly over my nightstand where my phone was attached to the charging cable. *There!* My fingers slipped over the phone's glass screen, and I pulled it to me, tearing it from the cable. My hands were numb as I swiped up and pressed the symbol for the torch. The beam of light lanced across the room and I spotlighted the dim corner where she stood.

"He told me to do it!" she cried, shielding her eyes from the glare. "He made me!"

My heart skipped a beat as I stared at the frail girl before me. She must have been around my age, eighteen or so. Her long dark hair knotted in sweat-drenched strands that clung to her neck. Dirt was smeared across her porcelain skin, hollowing her thin features.

"What's happened to you?" I murmured. "Are you hurt?"

She pressed her hands over her ears and shook her head wildly, eyes squeezed shut.

"I'll call 911," I stammered, losing the ability to move my hands.

She pressed her lips tightly together.

I considered shouting for help. Someone in the dorm block was bound to hear me. But my voice was trapped in my throat.

"What's your name?" I managed.

Tears began to spill down her cheeks, and she opened her eyes to meet my gaze.

I held my focus on her, trying to place if I'd ever seen her before. She stepped forward, away from the shadowed corner of my room, and into clearer view.

Her wide eyes shone like liquid gold. No a sign of white, just gold, with swollen black pupils.

"He told me I'd need to," she whispered. "I tried not to. I didn't want to."

I couldn't find the words to respond. My mind was whirling. Who was she? And what was she doing in my dorm room? Why couldn't I move?

"I tried to end it," she went on, "but I can't. He said I wouldn't be able to resist. He was right."

I felt like the only part of me that could still move was the heart thumping slowly in my chest.

She stretched her thin hand towards me and reached for my face. Her fingers trailed down my cheek. They were ice-cold; they burned to the touch.

Internally I was screaming, but on the outside, I was still, frozen. The torchlight lit her face from beneath her chin as she leaned in close to me. Suddenly her gaunt face and the shadows that the light created twisted her features in darkness.

"Close your eyes," she murmured.

On her command, my eyelids dropped, weighed down. I tried to move, to open my eyes, to shout for help, anything.

Then something pressed against my lips.

I lost grasp on reality as her kiss pressed deeper. I was pulled under; dragged down by an ice-cold wave. What followed, was a bolt of electric pain, as my very soul seemed to slip from my body.

My eyes shot open. I drew in a fractured breath. Her face was still close to mine, golden eyes brimming with sadness.

Then everything turned black.

I woke up breathless and drenched in sweat. Quickly, I sat up and looked around the room, half expecting the dream to be playing out before me like a bad horror movie. Morning light shone into my room, erasing all remnants of my nightmare.

As I came to, I responded to the shrill noise of my phone's alarm. It was still plugged in and charging on the bedside table where I'd left it the night before. It wasn't sealed in my hand, or tangled in my sheets. I looked to window, and that was closed now too, with no sign that it had ever been open at all.

I let out a ragged breath and raked my hands through my damp hair.

Three loud bangs tremored through my wall, spurring me to turn off my blaring horn of an alarm. I rolled out of bed and trudged around the room, looking for any sign of a mysterious raven-haired girl ever being in here. Of course, there was nothing.

Get a grip, Stef, I thought, rubbing the sleep out of my eyes. *Coffee. I need coffee. A lot of coffee.*

An abrupt knock on my door made me jump. I shrugged into the thick navy robe that mum had sent me in one of her many college care packages, then moved towards the door.

I'd barely had a chance to turn the lock before the door burst open. A brunette girl carrying two takeout coffee cups stood in my doorway. Phoebe.

Her nose wrinkled as she eyed me. "You look like shit," Phoebe said. She reached out with her free hand and flattened down some of my wayward hair.

I pushed her hand away. "Good morning to you, too, Phoebe," I said wryly. "I hope at least one of those is for me." I gestured to the two stacked coffee cups.

Phoebe handed me one, then strode into my room without invitation. Not that she needed an invitation. Her dorm was next door to mine, but I'd swear she spent more time in my room than her own.

"Fun night?" she asked.

"I've had the craziest dreams," I replied. I glanced at the small mirror hanging on my wall, assessing my reflection. My brown hair was a mess, and dark shadows hung beneath my thick lashes.

"I thought I heard noises coming from this room last night," Phoebe went on. She smirked as she planted herself on my unmade bed and swung her legs up onto the mattress. "I'm thinking of lodging a complaint about the construction of our dorms. Seriously, Stef, the walls are paper thin. All you have to do is a sneeze, and it sounds like a goddamn steam train passing through."

My mind wandered back to the phantom girl in my dream. "You heard noise coming from my room?" I frowned. "What did you hear?"

"You want me to demonstrate?" Phoebe giggled wickedly. "Shame on you! You know we aren't allowed *company* in our rooms after ten p.m.. University of Briarwood rules." She raised her hand in girl scout code, then took a swig of coffee.

I rolled my eyes. "Trust me; I didn't have *that* kind of company. I haven't seen Will since Monday, and I swear he wasn't with me last night." I'd been dating Will for a couple of months now, and things were going well. But not sneaking-him-into-my-dorm-after-hours kind of well. "I must have been talking in my sleep or something," I replied, brushing off the uncertainty.

She snorted. "Well, that must have been one hell of a good dream you were having!"

I took a long sip of coffee from my takeout cup and raised a brow.

"You don't look well, are you sure your good?" Phoebe's stare narrowed as she looked at me.

Phoebe was right, though. I looked like shit, and I felt even worse. My Grecian skin was two shades lighter than its usual sun-kissed hue.

"Maybe I'm getting sick," I said, rubbing my brow. "It's flu season, right?"

"Man-flu season more like," Phoebe said from where she sat on the bed. "So, does that mean you're gonna skip class today?"

I shook my head. "No. I'm just tired. Anyway, Professor Markell would kill me if I ditched again." At the start of the semester, I elected to major in Bio-Chemistry, which, as it happened, was not a class for coasters. I'd already earned myself an official warning about skipping too many lectures.

Phoebe glanced at my phone on the nightstand. "It's only eight-fifteen," she said. "Class doesn't start for forty-five minutes. What do you say we ditch this lukewarm crap and get a refresh?" She launched her takeout cup into the wastepaper basket where it landed with a thump. "Java Coffee House?"

I frowned at her. "You know we could just use the kettle in the communal kitchen," I said, thumbing towards the door. "We don't have to waste our money on hourly trips to Java all day."

Her jaw dropped. "You're going to turn down a beautiful; chocolate dusted Java latte for a limescale mug of Instant crap?"

She had me there.

Phoebe waited for me in the hall while I got dressed. I grabbed my Bio-Chem notebook and my phone and slipped out the door. Java was the leading coffee house on campus, and once we'd navigated the dorm block staircase and left the building, it was only a short walk across the gated acres of campus.

Outside in the fresh morning air, winter nipped at my skin. It hadn't snowed for a few days, but the remnants of slush were still evident across the stone path. Even on the stretches of grass surrounding the walkway were frozen memories of ice and snow.

As we walked, Phoebe held her phone in front of her; her earbuds jammed in as she caught up on her daily podcast, just like she did every morning. It didn't bother me that we didn't speak during our trek—actually, I appreciated the comfortable silence between us. Since meeting Phoebe at the start of the semester, I'd grown accustomed to her avid interest in angel healing and new age junk. I'd fast learnt not to interrupt the daily podcasts or ask questions; it was never a good idea to jump into *that* type of conversation this early in the morning.

As I adjusted the weight of my heavy backpack on my shoulder, I felt my phone buzz in my jeans pocket, but between the thick gloves and stiff denim, there was no way I was going to pull it out. Plus, it was most likely just Mum. She'd left for Greece with her girlfriend for the winter and was obsessed with texting me every morning since she'd arrived last week.

Are you eating healthily, Stef?
How are classes going, Stef?
What's the weather like, Stef?

I rolled my eyes at the thought of another Mum message. *How are you sleeping, Stef?* Was bound to come up sooner or later. And I wasn't ready to tackle that one. Beside me, I heard Phoebe's phone ping, followed by her moan of complaint as it distracted from the podcast.

She stopped walking abruptly.

"What's up?" I asked, stopping on the stone pathway and turning to face her. A couple of college seniors sidestepped past us.

"There's a new message on Dorm Block D group chat," Phoebe murmured, yanking the headphones from her ears. "Jeanie has been found..." She pressed her hand to her mouth. "Jeanie... she's dead."

CHAPTER TWO

Flashing blue lights reflected off Dorm Block D's brick walls. We stood amongst the ever-growing crowd of students, murmurs of death leaking through the winter breeze. Cold air bit at me and my face turned numb.

Blocking the entrance was an ambulance and two police cars parked up in from of our building, and police tape cordoning off the area.

Phoebe chewed her lower lip. "What the hell happened, Stef? We were just here." Her eye trained on one of the female officers standing guard, stopping those from leaving or entering the dorm.

I blew out a breath and ran my hand through my hair. "This can't be right. There has to be a mistake." It had been twenty minutes since we left the dorm and all Hell broke loose.

Phoebe checked her phone screen as our dorm chat message alert pinged in a steady rhythm. "People are asking if she killed herself, or if someone murdered her... No one has anything concrete yet." She groaned and slipped her phone back into her coat pocket. "I feel sick."

I gritted my teeth. I couldn't stop picturing the girl from my dream, bruised cheeks streaked with tears, long matted hair… Phoebe's voice tore me from my reverie.

"Apparently Tanner was the one who found her." Phoebe's gaze was trapped on her phone as she scrolled through the incoming messages.

"Tanner?" I winced at the thought. "Poor guy." I swallowed hard, and added, "Poor Jeanie."

Jeanie's room was across the hall from mine. I didn't know her that well, but from what I'd seen, she was a cool girl, smart and chatty. The idea that she'd died at our school, in our *building*, turned my stomach.

"Poor girl," I murmured again.

Briarwood was a small town. When I moved here for schooling, I loved that the little streets, local shops and bustling library where compact in a town of no more than a couple of thousand. So when things happen like this, which was a rare occasion, the news would spread to everyone in a matter of hours.

A hush fell over the crowd, and we all watched the doors to the building swing open. Tanner stepped out, escorted by two officers to one of the marked cop cars. Tanner's head was bowed as he slipped into the back of the vehicle.

Phoebe drew in a breath. "Why are they taking Tanner?"

My answer dropped in my stomach like a rock. Right before our eyes, the ambulance team carried out a body bag. Cries began to erupt around me and as we all stood motionless, watching our peer was carried away; never to return.

Dead.

I turned to Phoebe and followed her gaze to a window four stories up. Jeanie's window.

"It's okay, I understand," Phoebe murmured under her breath.

I turned to her. "What?"

She shook her head, then looked at me with a smile that didn't quite reach her eyes. "I said I don't understand," she said.

"I thought you said something else?, I prompted. "Are you sure your ok?"

"Oh." She pursed her lips. "I'm alright."

Phoebe wouldn't look at me. She kept her gaze lingering on Jeanie's window. The crowd was growing around us, filling with students who wanted to watch the drama. I caught a gaggle of girls crying into each other's arms as she mouthed Jeanie's name.

The air was thick with mourning.

Chapter Three

While everyone else had watched Jeanie leave Dorm Block D in a body bag, I'd watched her in her bedroom window. Her eyes had pierced through the frosted glass and the winter air where the onlookers huddled.

Someone killed me; the wind had carried Jeanie's otherworldly voice to my ears. I'd stared right back at her misted figure in the window, not quite there, but as there to my eyes, as her corporeal form had been in the body bag to everyone else.

"You can see me?" She had asked me through the channels of my mind.

I nodded my head, just enough to convey my answer to Jeanie's ghost, but not enough to make Stef beside me question the action.

Then Jeanie started talking at one hundred miles a minute. Her frantic voice flooded my mind and made my head throb.

"What happened to me?" she demanded. "Do you know what happened? The last thing I remember was waking up, and someone, something was in my room!"

I raised my hand ever so slightly, enough to signal to her, to urge her to stay calm.

She was talking fast. The dead ones often did. It seemed that dying filled spirits with adrenaline. It didn't help their stress when they find that someone could hear them, no less *see* them, that they had to get all of their unspoken thoughts out in one breath.

Jeanie stared down at me now from the fourth-floor window. "It burned," she relayed. "So much pain. I was being torn apart from the inside. Someone kissed me…"

Kissed? I exhaled into the cold air, barely hearing the sobs of the onlookers around me. I was as oblivious to them as they were of me and my private conversation with the dead girl.

This changed everything. It had 'supernatural' written all over it. I should have figured that out sooner. I could smell the stench in the air even before I'd heard the news. And there was only one breed I knew of who loved to depart with a brush of lust and touch. The Incubus. Darling little beasts.

"What am I supposed to do now?" Jeanie's ethereal voice had gone up an octave, and her translucent hands pressed to her heart. "I have finals coming up. Had finals!"

Finals? Really? If mum hadn't reprimanded me for playing with the newly deceased, I would have pointed out the irony. Jeanie's *final* happened already.

"Can you hear me?" she asked again, frantically. "I need you to hear me! I need you to help me!"

"It's okay," I whispered to the silvery figure in the fourth-floor window. "I understand."

Stef turned to me. "What?"

Damn. Never a good idea to talk to ghosts out loud. "I said I don't understand," I said. I was a lame liar. But what else was I supposed to do? Lying was better than the alternative. I mean, what would I even say if I told the truth anyway? *I'm a Guardian demon hunter, and I see dead people*? I'm not sure Stef would buy that one.

But Stef was freaked out. Everyone was. Death on campus was brutal. The question I wondered though, was what the hell was an Incubus demon doing on here in the first place?

Chapter Four

Conversation was non-existent between Phoebe and I as we sipped our coffees at Java, trying to act as though everything was normal. *Nothing* was normal. I felt cold, sick, and like darkness had fallen upon us, and I was afraid it would never leave.

I caught Phoebe's gaze; she'd been staring into space, lost in thought. "Are you okay?" I asked her, numbly.

"Yeah," Phoebe said with a long breath. "It's just…y'know?"

"Yeah," I agreed. "I know." I gazed out the window as the blizzard began to brew and students walked by with their heads bowed away from the snowfall.

Nearly an hour had passed since we'd watched Jeanie's body get carried away. The shock had hit us both, and time had started to blur.

Phoebe cleared her throat. "I bet it was one of those freak, unexplainable deaths," she said. "You know, one of those deaths where people just go to sleep and never wake up. Peaceful, and all."

"Maybe," I replied although I didn't believe that. And I sensed that she didn't, either.

My phone buzzed. I picked it up from the table and unlocked it. It was a mass message from the Dean of the university.

"All classes cancelled for the rest of the day," I relayed the text. I turned the screen towards Phoebe, and she read the announcement aloud.

"Students of Briarwood University are informed that all classes and proceedings are cancelled today, Wednesday, December 15th, and will resume tomorrow as normal. In light of this morning's events in Dorm Block D and the passing of a fellow student, please be advised that the university will be looking into the situation delicately. If anyone has any information on Jeanie Thompson and her whereabouts on Tuesday 14th December, please contact the Briarwood police department on extension 193. Students are reminded that the counsellor's office will remain open from 8 am to 6 pm."

"I knew something wasn't right about this," I muttered. "Why else would the Dean need information on Jeanie's whereabouts yesterday?"

"Okay," Phoebe conceded. "Something is off, but the police are on it, and I'm sure they'll get to the bottom of this."

My gaze wandered over the groups of students that filled the seats around us, many of whom were now looking at their phones, probably reading the same message that we were. I noticed a couple of guys around a table grinning and high-fiving about a day of cancelled classes. My chest tightened.

Phoebe rose from her seat. "I'll get us another coffee…"

I heard her voice, but everything around me seemed to have slowed down, muted.

Through the snow-speckled window, I saw a girl with long black hair and porcelain skin. My heart rate quickened, and a familiar panic spiked in my throat. Everything suddenly seemed muffled as the girl stared into Java's window, her eyes on me. It was *Her*.

She smiled and walked away.

I heard my chair clatter to the floor before I realised I'd jumped up. Ignoring Phoebe's calls I ran for the door, throwing it open to the awaiting winter air. I ran out onto the stone pathway, my gaze darting in every direction as I tried to find Her through the dozens of faces and bodies. There was no way she could have gotten out my sight so quickly.

I raised a hand to shield from the snowy downpour, but it didn't help. I could no longer see her.

"Stef!" Phoebe paced out of Java, pulling her scarf around her neck. "What has gotten into you!"

I blinked back at her in a strange daze. "I…I thought I saw someone…"

"Who?"

My gaze went back to the student passing by in the fluttery white blizzard.

"I'm not sure," I murmured.

Phoebe shivered and wrapped her arms around herself. "Okay, you're freaking me out. Let's go back inside." Her folded her hand over my arm.

But I couldn't tear my focus away from the campus grounds. Surely this couldn't be happening. It was just a dream.

I rubbed my hand over my brow. "I'm sorry, I—"

"You're freezing," Phoebe said, threading her arm through mine. "Come on."

I let Phoebe steer my back into Java. A few people were staring at me now. Even the barista's eyes were on me.

"Sit down. And drink," Phoebe said, nodding back towards our abandoned table. "Maybe you should stick to decaf this time."

I tried to laugh it off, but an ominous feeling brewed within me.

When spent the remainder of the day, battling the snow and visiting the few shops in the local town. There were not many, but it helped to kill time searching the bookshelves of Taunt Books and the sale racks of the local clothing chain. There were a few bars in town, most of which I have frequented, but a couple I stayed away from. I always felt a strange burning at the back of my neck when I passed one specific bar. Strange visitors would hang out in its dark rooms, sometimes for longer than a day. I would be caught dead near one of those.

Once Phoebe had burnt a hole in her pocket in the local mall, it was time to return to campus which was a short walk, mostly uphill. Snow came down even heavier this high, which meant by the time we reached our dorm our feet were frozen solid. We found that we were not allowed back in our dorm, so we opted to visit the school library were, thankful, an open fire was lit and ready for us.

When evening came around, we were permitted to return to Dorm Block D. Jeanie's death was already all over the local news, and even Will had gotten wind of it. He'd shown up at the dorm that evening to check on me. Will didn't study at the university. I'd met him in a bar on a bleary night out back in September, and since then he'd spent a lot of time hanging out on campus with Phoebe and me, watching movies or binging on Netflix boxsets.

"What are doing for Christmas break?" Will asked now as he placed a bowl of salted chips in front of me. "Your mum will be in Greece, right?"

"Yeah," I said. "I'll probably just hang out here over the holidays." I patted the sofa cushion in the common room.

Phoebe rolled her eyes. "Stef is staying with me for Christmas, aren't you?" She reached over and stole a handful of chips from the bowl. "My folks only live about half an hour outside of Briarwood."

"Thanks, Pheebs," I said with a quiet smile. We hadn't discussed that yet, but the dorm blocks were already starting to empty for the holidays, and I wasn't loving the idea of being alone on campus for Christmas.

"No biggie," she said with a wave of her hand. "What kind of friend would I be if I left you to fend for yourself on Christmas?" She paused and wrinkled her nose. "And don't call me Pheebs."

I grinned at her. She had a good point, with my mum away and my dad MIA, I was out of options. Mine and Will's relationship was still pretty new; too new to stay with him. I'd already met his family, and his mum had given me an open invite whenever I wanted to crash...but maybe it was a little too soon for a joint Christmas.

I liked Will, though. I liked him more than any of the guys I'd dated before. He was broad-shouldered and tall, over six feet. His auburn hair was always cropped short, accentuating his strong jawline and high cheekbones. But it wasn't just his looks that held my interest; he was thoughtful and sweet too. Sometimes we'd stayed up for hours just talking about the most random of things. Sometimes Netflix led to chilling, which was always a bonus.

I blushed, focusing on my chips. I was already devouring my third bowl already—I swear, my appetite today had been record-breaking. All day I'd felt hollow like nothing had been enough to fill the grumbling void inside my stomach. The more I ate, the more I wanted. I passed it off as a symptom of stress and made a mental note to Google search it later.

"I should head out," Will said, glancing at his watch. "It's nearly ten, and I promised I'd meet the guys in the bar tonight." He stood from the cushioned seat. I looked up as he placed his hands on either side of my face and leaned into me. With his lips inches from mine, he spoke,

"Have a good night. I'll call you tomorrow." Then he winked. Not caring that Phoebe was in the room—and probably cringing into her 7up—I leaned in and pressed a hungry kiss to his mouth.

I could feel Will's surprise beneath my lips, and he melted into me. I was hungry for him.

Hungry.

Something stirred in the pit of my stomach. A burning sensation, a fire. I needed more.

"*Fuck*!" Will pulled back from me suddenly. Frown lines creased on his brow.

"What's wrong?" I asked, breathless.

Will was rubbing his chest with his large hand, his face twisted in pain. "I don't know. Must be heartburn, or something." He tapped his fingers to his lips and pulled them away to check. "You almost bit my bottom lip off!"

"I didn't—" I began, but Phoebe interrupted.

Phoebe glanced up from her soda. "Call it karma for getting freaky right in front of me. Gross, by the way."

I threw her a quick smile but noticed something moving behind her. It was as if the very shadows of the room were alive, withering and bending before my eyes, darkening everything.

I blinked and rubbed my eyes, but the shadows kept dancing. I held my breath.

"I'll call tomorrow," Will finished, tapping his chest again before standing up to full high. "See you around, Phoebe."

"Um uh," she replied, mouthful.

Phoebe didn't care for Will much.

I smiled weakly to appease Will, then watched him walk through the churning darkness of the room to the exit. The shadows recollided from him as he left.

CHAPTER FIVE

I couldn't sleep. No matter how hard I tried, I couldn't stop my racing thoughts. Between Jeanie's death, and the phantom girl appearing outside Java, sleep was beginning to feel impossible.

After Phoebe and I sat through some junk rom-com about some nieve girl finding love in an airport, we'd returned to our respective bedrooms. Outside, any sign of the police intervention on Dorm Block D had disappeared. No more yellow tape cordoning off the entrance, or flashing blue lights projected onto the brickwork. Just silence.

My phone buzzed on the nightstand.

I gritted my teeth. I swear, if phone lit up one more time, then it too was about to meet its untimely end. I rolled over, tilting the screen to see the next influx of gossip spilling down the message thread. The latest was about Tanner. No one had heard from him since he'd left with the police, which, according to the rumour mill, meant he was a cold-blooded murderer, locked up in a cell awaiting trial.

Bullshit. Tanner wasn't a murderer. He was part of my Bio-Chem class, and I'd worked with him on a few projects in the past two months. He was a nice guy; soft-spoken and book smart.

I switched my phone off, watching the power and life slip from the device.

Tap…tap…tap.

My eyes shot open from my light sleep. Something was hitting the window pane, rattling the glass in slow thuds.

I flipped on the lamp and jumped out of bed, then paced across the room. Drawing the curtains apart, I cupped my hands on the glass and looked out into the moonlit night. The windowpane frosted which blurred the view beyond it.

I startled as something else hit the frosted pane right in front of my face.

My fingers sealed around the latch, and I pushed the window open, leaning out into the frigid air.

"Cut it out. Are you fucking crazy!" I shouted towards the stone thrower.

From the fourth storey window, it was hard to make out the silhouette standing on the dark pavement below. But the crest of a raven-haired head tilted upward and a girl—*the* girl—looked up at me.

The sight of her seemed to paralyse me. She waved a fragile hand, as if she and I were just old friends, and that I was expecting her visit. Maybe, on some level, I was. But I didn't wave back.

The moon shadows began to bend and curve around her, morphing her blackened tresses into a trick of darkness. And just like that, she was gone. Now I stared at the empty pavement, the midnight darkness making me question if she had ever been there at all, or if she'd moved behind the trees without my noticing.

I staggered back into the room and pulled the window closed, turning the handle up hard. This couldn't be real. I was sleeping; I had to be.

There was a bang on my door, and I let out a noise somewhere between a scream and a choke. I pressed my hand to my mouth. I couldn't move—not to the window or towards the door.

The knock came again. Taking a solid step forward, I turned the handle and opened the door.

When I saw Phoebe standing in the outer corridor, my breath escaped in a rush.

"Someone was throwing stones at my window!" I hissed.

Phoebe's brown hair was in a messy ponytail, her plaid bed clothes hanging off her.

"I heard you shouting," she whispered, glancing furtively along the empty corridor. "With what happened to Jeanie I wanted to check on you."

I looked at her and then dark corridor beyond my room. "Just come in," I said, stepping aside for her. My heart was still racing.

"What is going on, Stef?" she asked in a hoarse voice. "You've been acting weird all day. Now, this." She waved her hands. "If you are worried about something then tell me. That's what I'm here for."

I sat on the chair beside my desk, dropping my head into my hands. "Phoebe, I think I'm losing my mind. I'm…" I let out a ragged breath. "Since last night I have seen things. A girl."

To my surprise, she didn't snort out a laugh or make some sarcastic comment about Will. She just calmly said, "You're tired. It's been a long, crazy day—"

"No," I cut her off. "I don't think that's it. It felt real. I'm seeing *her* everywhere. Outside on the street, at Java, and even in here." I gestured to the corner of my small room, where the girl had occupied my nightmare.

Phoebe stared back at me. "You have to give me a little more than this, Stef," she said. "Who are you seeing?"

"That's just it," I exclaimed, "I don't know! I dreamed about her last night… or, at least, I thought it was a dream until I saw the same girl standing outside Java this morning, and then again just now outside my window."

Again, Phoebe glanced at the window, our reflections mirrored off the pane.

"She's gone," I said. "She disappeared. She was there, and then she was gone."

Phoebe groped for words. "Maybe you're overtired, stressed, worried about classes and—"

"No." I pressed my knuckles to my mouth. "Phoebe, you have to believe me."

"I do, Stef," she murmured. "I do." She blew out a breath. "Your dream. What happened?"

"She appeared in my room," I recounted. "Right there in that corner. She was all scratched up and muddy." Phoebe's eyes followed my finger to the corner of the room, where the paint was peeling from the plasterboard. "Then she walked towards me," I went on, swallowing, "and I just lay in bed. I couldn't move."

Phoebe held her breath.

"And she kissed me," I said. "That's all I remember. Well, that, and the pain. It felt like I was dying, really dying, like my insides slipped out of me. Even when I woke up, that feeling was still there, somewhere." My head hummed at the memory. "Then when we were at Java yesterday, I thought I saw her—"

"And that's why you ran outside," Phoebe supplied.

"Yes. But *she* wasn't there."

"So, you think she came back again tonight?"

"Someone was throwing something at my window," I explained. "When I looked it was her. She was just standing there on the pavement. She fucked waved at me, Phoebe!"

Phoebe sat motionless on the bed, her face pinched.

"You think I'm making this up, don't you?" I asked, not ready for the answer. "You think I'm losing my shit. I probably am."

35

"No," she half-laughed. "You're not losing your shit. It's just...a lot to take in." She stood up and trotted to the window. I turned my head away from the burst of night air, as the window swung open. Goosebumps prickled over my bare arms.

"Well," Phoebe said finally, pulling the window shut. "If Mystery Girl was there, she's certainly not anymore. It's dead out there." I winced at her word choice. "You need to get some sleep," she concluded. "And if she does come back. She will have me to answer to."

CHAPTER SIX

I'd seen the shadows lurking around Dorm Block D, and it didn't take long to figure out that they were demonic. The stench alone was enough to leave a mark. It was a little tricky distinguishing exactly *which* demon force had decided to settle here. Judging by Jeanie's account of her final moments, and now Stef's mystery girl, my money was on an Incubus—or the feminine form, Succubus. It's the only demonic being that has the power to spread so much lust.

In my eighteen years, my run-ins with the Incubus breed were relatively few and far between. But, damn, the encounter I'd had was enough to chew me up, spit me out, put me in a blender and leave me for kibble— emotionally, at least. Physically I'd managed to come out unscathed. Which was more than I could say for most people who encountered an Incubus.

It had happened a little after my fifteenth birthday, I was a Junior in high school at the time, and my parents had only recently let out on the field alone. I'd been training as a Guardians for as long as I could remember. Mum and Dad were a little more cautious that their only child—a flimsy waif of a daughter— was going out on demon hunts alone. So by fifteen, I toughened up enough to earn my stripes.

I was patrolling the Briarwood cemetery one Saturday night when I met my first distraction. I'd been sitting on one of the headstones outside the mausoleum, just waiting for something to go down. It was a full moon, a beacon in the otherwise black and hazy sky, so I was hoping for some action. Anything. A vampire resurrection, or a nice werewolf turn, something easy for an autumn weekend. But other than a couple of translucent spirits weaving through the plots, it was dead.

Then *he* showed up.

"You shouldn't be out here alone." That's what he'd said to me.

I turned on my headstone seat and arched an eyebrow at the boy approaching in the darkness. He wasn't a vampire or a werewolf; he was just a boy. Perhaps a little older than me, brown hair and pale golden eyes.

"What are you doing out here, anyway?" He walked right up to me, giving me this look. This infuriating, *you're just a girl,* kind of look.

I tapped the wooden stake that was wedged into my back pocket, feeling the smooth elm point. "I'm just enjoying the night," I said, "looking for something to kill." I met his gaze. "Problem?"

He smirked. "No. Not really. I was trying to do you a favour, that's all." He stuffed his hands into his jacket pockets and shrugged his shoulders. "I'm sure there are a few other creatures out here looking for something to kill, too." His head titled. "You look like a nice something to kill."

"Thank you," I said.

He almost laughed. "Oh no, thank *you*, fresh meat."

I wrinkled my nose. "You have such a way with words."

He grinned, looking particularly boyish and handsome. "I'm glad you noticed."

I bet you are, I thought, assessing him with my steady gaze.

"So, you're one of them?" he asked.

"One of who?"

"The do-gooders," he elaborated, smirking. "The Guardians." His tone was unbearably mocking. These types always mocked us—until they ended up as bones and dust.

"Yes," I replied coolly. "And I presume you are one of *them*," I returned. "The do-baders. The ones whom innocents must be *Guarded* against?"

"Is that even a word?" He mimed tipping a proverbial hat. His leaned against a tombstone, regarding me carefully. "So, now what?" he asked.

"I kill you, or you kill me, whichever comes first." But I didn't move. He smiled, so I smiled back. God-only-knows why we were laughing. We were supposed to be killing.

"What's your name, Guardian?" he asked.

"Phoebe."

He extended his hand to me, and I accepted it. Our skin fused together, ice-cold and red-hot all at the same time. His fingers tightened around me, not in a threatening way, just in a...*way*.

"I'm Sam," he said.

And that was how it started.

Chapter Seven

Phoebe's family were the eccentric type. They believed in spirits, and 'The wisdom of the Tarot', as Phoebe put it. They lived on the outskirts of Briarwood, about fifteen miles from campus. I enjoyed our visits to see them, even if Pheobe didn't. She would always try and persuade me that we didn't need to visit.

I always got my own way. Especially if I used the 'I haven't seen my mum for a long time, and I miss her," look.

We pulled up outside their gated manor in Phoebe's old Chevy truck.

"Home sweet home," she said with a faint smile.

Before us, black iron gates had rusted, and moss had spread over the surface. The crumbling walls beside them had seen better days. Every time we visited it seemed another brick was missing.

Once Phoebe killed the engine we climbed out of the truck. I went first, pushing the gate open with a shoulder. The merciless groan as it swung wide was unpleasant.

We trudged along the driveway, through the flanking front lawn which was rich with dewy grass and a myriad of tropical flowers and horticulture. Holy had grown from the bushes beside us, flexing the silver snowed ground with balls of red.

I stayed behind Phoebe as we ascended the porch steps leading up to a looming grey manor house, with old stone columns rising tall into the misted sky. The house was straight out of a Charles Dickens novel. From the outside, it was depressing and dull. But I knew not to judge its exterior on the inside was a different matter.

This wasn't my first visit to Phoebe's family home. My first time here had been...interesting. I'd spent most of the time coughing into my sleeve on the thick fumes of burning incense and hanging spices, and when Phoebe's mum, May, had offered me a drink, I'd ended up with a glass of water sprinkled with sage and rose petals. But by the time I'd left after that first visit, I'd fallen in love with the rabbit warren of rooms, each one alive with a unique colour and scents.

Today's visit was May's idea. According to Phoebe, her mum requested we visit immediately. And judging by the unease in Phoebe's tone when she'd mentioned it, I was starting to guess that *being summoned* wasn't necessarily a good thing.

I waited on the front porch while Phoebe dug out her old brass skull key from her shoulder bag. I stared down at a pot of nettles that May used for brewing teas, taking a deep breath of the scents of lavender and spice from the many potted plants. Honestly, I was struggling to focus on anything but the pounding pressure building inside my head and the pangs of hunger in my stomach that I *still* couldn't seem to satisfy.

The front door swung open before Phoebe had managed to jam her key into the lock.

May stood in the doorway, wild silver hair fastened at the crown of her head. "This saddens me," she murmured huskily. "Get inside before the cold kills you *first*."

Phoebe followed her mother into the house, and I trailed behind. My headache gave another agonising thud as I stepped beneath the white sage garland suspended above the door frame.

"Interesting," May muttered, glancing over her shoulder at me as she led us into the long, plum-coloured corridor. "Very interesting indeed."

I tried not to frown back at her. *Interesting?* What was interesting? Had she meant me? Suddenly I felt incredibly conspicuous.

We carried on along the corridor. Ornate oil painting depicting generations of Phoebe's family members hung from the walls, scattered between sconce candles and string beads. Our trio of footsteps fell in sync as we moved deeper along the flagstone floor.

Suddenly I felt as though I were underwater, hearing only muted echoes, buried with the shipwrecked gates and drowning somewhere beneath the surface.

May came to a stop before an oak door and gestured into the room. "Take a seat in the drawing room," she said in her raspy accent. "I'll get you some chew bark for that headache."

I raised my eyebrows at Phoebe as May left us alone in the drawing room.

"How did she know about my headache?" I mouthed.

Phoebe flipped her palms. "She knows everything. And you are holding your head like it's about to explode."

We took our seats on the crushed velvet wingchairs and stared into the crackling log fire. The heat pulsing from the flames began to warm my cold skin. I rubbed my hands together.

"So," I said, returning my gaze to Phoebe, "are you ever going to tell me?"

She sat upright, rigid in her seat. "Tell you what?"

"Whatever it is that you're not telling me."

She pressed her lips together.

"Does your mum know about my dream?" I asked. "I am guessing you told her." I winced as the pain crashed a little louder inside my skull.

Phoebe stared down at her fingernails for a second. "I didn't need to tell her," she said. "Didn't you hear me before? She already knows. She knows everything."

I scoffed out a laugh.

"Everything," Phoebe repeated meaningfully.

I arched an eyebrow. "I find that hard to believe."

Phoebe sighed. "What can I say, mumma May's mind works in mysterious ways."

The sound of the drawing room door opening made us both jump. Phoebe's father, Michael, stepped into the room and smiled broadly at us. He loped across the room, his willowy frame casting a long shadow in the firelight. His grey hair pulled into a high bun. He wore a frayed cardigan with a pair of glasses hanging over his chest on a silver chain.

"Dad," Phoebe greeted him as he planted a kiss on her forehead.

"Hey, kiddo," he replied warmly. He turned to me and extended his hand. "Good to see you again, Stef. How are classes going?"

"Okay," I said, returning his smile. "Bio Chem is pretty intense, but Phoebe's a good lab partner."

She grinned. "The *best* lab partner," she corrected raising an index finger.

Michael chuckled. "And your mum?" he asked, his eyes still on me. "I hear she's in Greece?"

"Yeah," I said. "Mum's planning on moving out there with her new girlfriend."

"Ah, well, it's a beautiful country," Michael said. "I hardly blame her." He cleared his throat. "And how about your father, Stef? Where is he?"

Phoebe grimaced. "*Dad!*"

Michael blinked back at her. "What? It's a simple question, Phoebe."

"Dad, you're being rude," she said through clenched teeth.

I lifted my palm in peace. "No, it's fine," I told Michael. "Unfortunately, I don't know where my father is. I've never met the guy." I felt my cheeks burn as I said the words aloud. It was a painful thing to admit. I had to

45

admit; it was an odd question. In all the times I had seen Phoebe's parents, my father had never been brought up in conversation.

"Oh." Michael rubbed his jawline, his fingers moving over the white stubble on his chin. "I'm sorry to hear that."

"It's fine," I said. "I'm over it." I had to be over it. I had no other choice. Anyway, as nice as it was to chat with Phoebe's parents, I got the feeling that I wasn't *summoned* here for small talk.

On cue, May walked into the room, carrying a brass tea tray. "Drink up," she said, placing the cups on the coffee table between us as Michael took a seat by the fire. "And here," she said, handing me a small strip of what looked like tree bark. "It's willow bark. Chew on it, and it will help ease the pain." She simpered and placed her index finger on my temple. "For now, anyway."

Warily I took the bark and placed it between my lips. I bit down on it, and to my surprise, the pain receded a fraction.

"So," May began as she sank into the remaining chair around the fireplace. "How are classes going?"

"Mum," Phoebe said with a groan. "Can we just get to the point already?"

May inhaled. "Right," she said, pursing her lips. "Well, Stef, I think you know why you're here."

Between the pain in my head, and the insatiable hunger and the bark now balanced between my teeth, my patience for guessing games was a little lacking. I pulled the bark out of my mouth. "I don't mean to be forward, May, but I'd rather you just tell *me* why I'm here."

She smiled back at me. "I must say, I admire your directness, my dear. I can only respect you with the same address." She leaned back in her seat, glancing between Michael and Phoebe before her azure eyes returned to me. "I must tell you, Stef; the stones have been pointing to a change for you. Do you have an idea what that might be?"

All three of them stared at me now, an intense and nervous stare that made the hairs on the back of my neck bristle. "I…I don't know."

"Anything unusual?" Michael asked.

I sat stiffly, unsure of how to broach my worries about the phantom girl. It wasn't that I thought they would judge me—of anyone, they seemed open to believing anything out of the ordinary. It was more than I was unsure of what exactly I was supposed to say.

Fortunately, Phoebe answered for me. "Oh come on!" she urged her parents. "You called us over here. What do you know? What can you tell Stef?"

What can they tell me? That seemed like odd wording, even for Phoebe.

I expected May and Michael to give some mystical answer. But they didn't. May briefly looked at her husband and turned to me with an eerie smile.

"I'm not sure," she said. "The signs are showing me hints, but… Anyway, I'm sure you'll find your answers soon."

Phoebe dropped her head in her hands and laughed, but it was a cold and bitter sound.

"Is that it, then?" Phoebe asked, standing abruptly. "Are we done? We came over for that!"

"For now," May said. "Phoebe maybe you should take Stef back to campus to sleep off that headache."

I stood up, and May embraced me in a hug. When she broke away, she met my eyes, holding my stare. "I hope you feel better soon."

"Uh, yeah," I said. "Thanks. I guess I'll see you next week for the holidays."

May's face pinched slightly; as if my comment saddened her.

"Ah, yes," Michael agreed as he rose to his feet too. "Phoebe mentioned that you'd be staying here during school break."

"Wonderful," said May as she ushered me back towards the corridor. "Phoebe," she called suddenly. "May I speak with you *alone* for a moment."

Phoebe threw me an apologetic glance as we hovered in a drawing-room off the corridor. Leaving me alone.

"I'll wait by the car." I cooed.

I didn't waste any time in putting distance between myself and the house. I let myself out through the front door and paced quickly along the path towards the iron gates. When I turned back, I could see their silhouettes in the huge bay window. Phoebe and May were standing face to face with each other. I couldn't hear the words from out here, but whatever they were talking about seemed animated. Hands and arms were waving then

Phoebe tipped her head back. I'd never seen her this angry. They didn't look my way until Phoebe walked off and May called for her, this time her voice echoing in the quiet street.

Phoebe stormed out of the house; her head bowed as she paced along the path towards the gates.

"Everything okay?" I asked.

"Yeah, fine," she muttered. She ducked past me and opened the truck where we'd left it parked on the curb.

"Phoebe?" I went after her, slipping into the passenger's seat and closing the door behind me. "You are angry, what did you May say to you?" My breath misted the windscreen.

"Nothing." She turned the key in the ignition; the engine started to purr.

"Because if your parents don't want me to coming over for the holidays—"

"No," she said, her eyes finding mine now. "It's not that. It's nothing. It's fine."

Yeah, sure seemed fine, I thought.

CHAPTER EIGHT

No, no, no.

That's about all I could think as I drove away from my parents' house. *No.*

Of course, I'd known why my mum and dad had been so keen to see Stef; I wasn't a complete idiot. But naively I'd been hoping that they'd have a different take on the situation. After all, they were the experts. I was just a novice. A screw-up novice.

I knew what my parents were thinking too, that this was my fault. It was *my* fault that Stefan was in this mess. And it was all because of that goddamn demon bastard.

I cringed as the memories crawled back to the forefront of my mind. I didn't want those memories back. I wanted them buried. I wanted all of it buried. I'd messed up, and now Stef was paying the price.

"Sam?" I called into the darkness.

On my command, he'd slithered out from the shadows of the cemetery in a whirl of smoke.

I trotted between the headstones and met him as he approached. I threw my arms around him.

"We have to stop meeting like this," he murmured into my ear as his arm snaked around me, drawing me closer to him.

I rose to my tiptoes and kissed his lips, shivering as he kissed me back, his arms locking tighter around me.

One...two...three... and then he pulled away, stepping back. Just like he always did. Just like he always had to do.

I inhaled slowly, feeling the sensation return to my body. I was numb when I was with Sam; I guess that was the power of the Incubus.

"We really *shouldn't* keep meeting like this," I mirrored his words, but my tone was far more serious than he had been. What the hell was I thinking? My parents would have pulled me out of field duty, revoked my privileges, and sent me off to some stuffy reform school if they had any idea what their newbie fifteen-year-old daughter was doing on Saturday nights in Briarwood Cemetery.

But since the day I'd met Sam, I hadn't been able to stay away from him. I hadn't been able to resist the urge to see him, and it seemed that he was suffering from that same internal struggle. So, every Saturday night for the past three months, we met at Maura Bishop's headstone, and we kissed, and talked, and kissed some more, and then restrained ourselves, because...well, he was an Incubus, which meant that we were one moment of passion away from my death. Or his. Depending on who struck faster.

Sam wound his fingers through my hair, his eyes finding mine in the moonlight.

"I missed you," he said.

"I missed you, too," the words came out in a rush. I had missed him. Between the gruelling drag of Monday to Friday, the longing only intensified. It was as though a little piece of him had transported into me through our lips, and now it tugged at my ribcage when we were apart, as though it were trying to find its way back to him. I wouldn't have described myself as a *romantic*, but this wasn't romance, this was chemistry, biology, and I was afraid that the more I allowed the fire to burn, the harder the flame would be to extinguish.

"I came to your school yesterday," he said, sitting on Maura's grave and leaning against the headstone. His arm covered up half the inscription on her stone, fragment her legacy. It now reads *In memory of Maura —devoted— died.*

I sank down beside him on the dewy ground. "You came to my school? Why?"

He smirked up at the moon. "I don't know," he murmured. "I guess I just wanted to see you in the daytime."

I felt my cheeks grow hot. "You did? I didn't see you."

"You Guardians," he replied, laughing, "you think you're good at your job. You can't even sense when a Demon is twenty feet away from you."

I swatted him. "Why didn't you come over to me?" My heart started beating faster. This was dangerous territory. It was one thing meeting in darkness when I was deliberately out looking for Demons like him—albeit to kill them, not kiss them—but another thing to meet in daylight. In the hours when I was alive and real, as opposed to existing in this pocket of a dreamlike world that didn't truly exist beyond the perimeters of midnight and dawn.

He tilted his face to look at me, and a gentle breeze moved through the strands of his deep brown hair. "I wanted to see you. You were talking to a guy, a scrawny kid, and I wanted to kill him."

I rolled my eyes.

"What?" he said, the picture of innocence. "I *didn't* kill him. I wanted to, I could have, but I didn't."

"Still a little over the top."

"They get you for the entire week," he said, pursing his lips into what could have been a smile, but seemed more like a grimace. "They see you for five days. That's seven daylight hours, five times a week. I don't even know you in the day—"

"Bright lights can be very unforgiving," I joked. But he wasn't smiling anymore.

"I want more," he said, tapping his palm on the earth beneath us. "I want you, all of you, daytime, nigh-time, all the time."

My pulse was racing, I could feel the blood pumping frantically through my veins, and I was afraid that he could feel it too, somewhere in his consciousness. I was afraid that it was driving him wild. "No," I murmured. "Sam, we agreed. Seeing you like this isn't right, this isn't normal—"

"To hell with normal. We weren't normal, to begin with,"

"My family—"

"To hell with families," he choked. "My family shut the door on me the day I turned. I don't have a family."

I held his gaze. "But I do, Sam," I said, as gently as I possibly could. "And my family would kill you if they found out. They wouldn't think twice about it, and you know that."

"It's worth the risk," he said, shrugging.

My heart gave a heavy thump. The fact that Sam was even saying such a thing showed how lost and broken Sam's world is. In truth, Sam was alone. Nothing had value anymore; he had nothing to lose—including, it seemed, his life.

"*I* can't risk it," I said. "I won't. Your life is important to me. *You* are important to me."

He threaded his fingers through mine; his eyes cast down to the blades of grass beneath us. "Okay," he said. "Then we'll keep meeting in secret. They don't have to find out."

"Saturday nights," I said.

"Saturday nights," he echoed. Then he kissed me. *Once, twice.* Then he pulled away.

For a moment he was quiet, we both were, then he turned to me and said, "Don't give up on me. Not yet."

"I won't," I whispered.

"I can be more," he murmured. "I don't have to kill to survive. It's just an urge, and I can resist it." He pressed his lips together, obstinate like even now he was fighting an impulse inside of himself. "Just wait," he said. "You'll see. I can be more than this. I can be more to you than this." He extended his hands to the darkness enveloping the cemetery.

I held my breath. I wanted more; daytime, night-time, all the time. But I was scared to say the thing that frightened me most, the reality of what this was. All it would take was one kiss too many, one touch too far, and I was either dead or turned.

Guardians and Demons don't fall in love. There were reasons; I just had to remember them.

Sam had been turned a few years earlier by some hungry newbie Succubus whose kill had gone wrong, filling him with demonic molecular cells, doing to him what he may one day do to me. He was frozen now, eternally seventeen, eternally golden-eyed and lusting for souls, and death, and sex. And I was at his mercy because I was hooked on him.

Now, then, and forever.

CHAPTER NINE

By the time we arrived back at campus after our visit to Phoebe's family home, my shoulders felt locked in tension. Whatever had happened between Phoebe and her mum had followed us the entire way back. Phoebe had been unnaturally quiet on the drive home, submerged into private thoughts that made her brow furrow as she drove. She parked up on campus. It had snowed since we left, coating the ground with an unblemished layer of white powder.

We stepped out of the truck and began wading through the snow towards the dorms.

I studied Phoebe's profile as we walked. I wished she'd talk to me, tell me what the argument was between her and May—it didn't take a genius to figure out that it'd had something to do with me.

I cleared my throat. "Hey," I said, drawing Phoebe's attention to me. Her eyes snapped to mine as if she'd only just realised I was walking alongside her. "I feel like I've done something to upset you?"

"Of course you haven't." She forced out a laugh. "Listen, can we just put today behind us. My parents can be such kooks. I've told mum to cut it out, or we will both not visit for Christmas."

I summoned a smile. "Phoebe…if there's something wrong, you'll tell me, won't you?"

Another false laugh. "Sure."

I blew out a breath. "Okay." I decided to change tack. "Do you wanna stop by Java?" I asked, pointing to where the wooden walkway branched off in the direction of the coffee house. "I could do with a caffeine fix and food. I swear I feel like I'm eating my stomach lining at this point."

Phoebe paused, looking at me than Java. "Um, actually, I was thinking of going back to my room for a while. I've got an assignment to finish before Christmas break…"

Since when did Phoebe prioritise coursework over coffee?

"Oh," I said. "Need any help?"

"No. You go." She gestured to the homely lights shining out from Java's bay windows. "How about I meet you there in an hour?"

It was a compromise, I supposed.

"Okay," I agreed. "If you're sure…"

"Yeah. I just need an hour to finish off this assignment."

"Right."

"And then I'll meet you." She was fumbling over her words, acting very un-Phoebe. But what was I meant to do? Drag the truth out of her. If she wanted alone time, I could hardly say no.

"See you later," I finished at last, and we turned to go our separate ways.

I traipsed through the snow towards Java and ducked inside the brightly lit café. The heating vents were blasting out warm arm, tinged with the scent of freshly brewed coffee and pastries. Half of the seats were already taken up by students; their heads dipped as they focused on the paperwork scattered across their tables. I found a quiet wingchair by the window and shrugged out of my jacket. As I flattened it over the arm of the chair, I withdrew my phone from the pocket and checked the screen.

One new message from Will, telling me he'd be at the bar late tonight, and one from my mum, with pictures from her day trip to Santorini.

Looks great! I replied to Mum, keeping my tone breezy, so she didn't catch on to any underlying tension. *Love the pic of you and Debs on the waterfront. I miss you.* I deleted the last line and rewrote; *I'm glad you're having a good time.*

After that, I braced myself to check the dorm group chat. There was a string of notifications, undoubtedly more gossip and conspiracy theories surrounding Jeanie, all of which I'd avoided looking at so far.

Swallowing the dryness in my throat, I opened up the message thread.

Just as I'd expected, names of people in Block D ran down the screen, all discussing Jeanie and what had happened. I scrolled through them until I reached the bottom, where I noticed people had started talking about Tanner.

Apparently, the cops have let Tanner go, someone wrote.

And there was a reply from another name I didn't recognise: *Yeah, it's true. I saw him this morning. He looked like shit. His dad picked him up from campus, and he's gone back home for Christmas break. I think he needed to get away from this place.*

Did you talk to him??

Yeah, the guy replied. *He's pretty messed up about it all. He said he burst into Jeanie's room because she wasn't responding to him. He thinks he saw some girl standing over the bed, and then he swears the girl just vanished.*

My stomach knotted. Had a girl been in Jeanie's room that night? The same night I'd dreamed about her.

I returned to the message thread.

What, like, she disappeared? Someone else wrote. *It sounds like Tanner's lost his mind!*

I know, right? But that's what he said.

Who was the girl?

Tanner didn't say. Not that it matters. He is just trying to cover his tracks I'm sure.

Suddenly I couldn't breathe.

PHOEBE

Chapter Ten

What mum had told me was not good. I couldn't shake it from my mind as I drove back. Even looking at Stefan was hard.

Stefan was changing. Putting everything he had told me together only solidified that into a fact. How could I tell him?

I slipped into my dorm room and pulled the door shut behind me. My hands trembled as I jostled open my dresser drawer and fumbled around for my deck of Tarot cards that I'd buried beneath my clothes

Personally, I'd always thought the Tarot cards were just a dumb parlour trick. But I was willing to try anything, and the usually worked to get a little insight at least.

I lit a candle and set it down on the floor in the centre of my room, then planted myself cross-legged in front of it.

I drew in a breath and began to shuffle, thinking only of Stef as I let the cards slip between my fingers, their silken surface cold against my skin.

Okay, foresight, let's see what you've got.

I spread the cards facedown across the floor, then selected one from the arched arrangement.

I flipped it over to see the image.

I'd been hoping for something a little less foreboding.

The grim reaper stared back at me, black cape pulled high over his hollow face, and a beady-eyed crow perched on his shoulder.

Death, I thought.

"Had you expected anything else?" a voice came from across my room.

I didn't bother looking up; I already knew who it was. "Do-over," I said, gathering up the cards for a second try.

She scoffed out a laugh.

This time, I looked up, frowning at her. Jeanie, last seen in the window of her crime-scene dorm, was now standing next to my pine wardrobe, with a strange silkiness to her faded appearance. She was eyeing me sceptically. It bugged me.

"There are no do-overs," she said, haughtily. "It's already done."

I grimaced and resumed shuffling the deck. "Not necessarily. Anyway, the death card only means change. That's not a bad thing."

"Then why the need for a do-over?"

I decided to ignore her—but I could feel her eyes on me as I fanned the cards out across the carpet again.

Come on, happy, cheery image of positivity, I willed.

I selected a card. And there *he* was again. Grimreaper in all his morbid glory.

"You know they're coming for Stef," she said. "The same ones who got me, they're coming for Stef."

I gritted my teeth. "I'll stop them. I'll figure out a way to reverse this."

She laughed again. "I have learnt a lot in death," she mocked me. "Listened and watched. Stalked and followed. I've heard them. The girl. The one who did this. He is angry with her you know. Very angry. Said it was a mistake. Said I was the wrong one. I hope they do kill him. It is all Stefan's fault." She pressed her wispy fingers to her pellucid chest.

I didn't respond. I just scooped up the deck and began shuffling again. Spirits always seeped into anger and denial. What they didn't know was it only kept them tethered to this dimension; stopping them from moving on.

"Nothing to say?" Jeanie called my attention back to her. "How will you stop the father of them all?"

"Leave." My voice was firm.

"Wouldn't you be better off figuring out how to end them? To end Stef before the change is complete?"

I kept shuffling, refusing to meet her glassy eyes.

"They're coming here, you know," she murmured. "I can feel it. They're on their way."

For a long moment, I was silent, just breathing steadily in and out.

"It's true," she said. "It won't be long."

I dropped the cards onto the carpet and rose to my feet.

Turning to the angered spirit, I pushed my hands sending the ball of light I'd kept buried towards her.

"I said *leave*."

Jeanie burst into a whisper of light and dust.

Chapter Eleven

An hour and a half had passed in Java, and still, Phoebe was a no-show. I'd already drained two coffees and was too wired to take on another one, even if she showed up now.

I'd already tried to call her a couple of times, but she wasn't picking up. I tried texting her instead.

Phoebe? I'm in Java, are we meeting here or what?

No response.

With a sigh, I rose to my feet and shrugged into my coat. What was the point in waiting around here any longer? I'd officially been stood up.

I left Java and began along the pathway back to the dorm blocks. There was something eerie about the campus; maybe it was down to the fact that everything was covered in a white blanket of fresh snow. Or maybe it was because the entire plot was suddenly empty. Most of the live-in students had already gone home for the holidays, and for the first time all semester, I found myself totally and utterly alone.

A sudden chill moved through me. But it wasn't the solitude that made the hairs on my arms bristle—it was the *company*. I wasn't alone. Someone walked behind me. I didn't turn around, not at first, I only listened to the slow, heavy footsteps crunching behind me.

I picked up my pace. I was acting paranoid, running from nothing but a passing stranger.

I snuck a glance over my shoulder. And there *he* was, a man, too old to be a student, too young to be a teacher.

I wasn't focusing on the sludgy path ahead as I rounded the corner into a tunnel of silver birches. Suddenly a woman was standing in front of me, her platinum hair moving slowly in the cold breeze. I flinched at the sight of her.

"Hello there," she purred, blocking my way. Her deep crimson eyes bore into me, somehow rendering me motionless. There was no white in her eyes. Only red. She grabbed my arm, her grip exceeding the appearance of her lithe frame. "I must admit, you look like a nice choice."

Another hand clamped down on my shoulder—the man who had been trailing me. My heart leapt into my throat.

Before I knew it, I was being dragged into the thick of trees, stumbling as I tried to keep my footing.

My head smacked against a tree trunk as the man knocked me down into the snow. Through bleary vision, I watched him slink back into the darkened web of trees.

I gasped for breath as the woman fixed her ruby stare at me.

"Who are—" I doubled over in pain as the tow of her leather boot impacted with my stomach.

She grabbed a fistful of my hair and yanked my neck back. Her breath smelled of honeysuckle as she whispered into my throat, "Shut your mouth, New Blood. You don't get to talk in my presence."

The man resurfaced through the snow-capped branches, and now he was dragging Phoebe along with him. She was fighting against him, but he held her tightly.

"Phoebe," I choked. I looked up at him, pleadingly. He sneered sinuously back at me, and for the first time, I noticed that his eyes were the same crimson hue as the women.

Phoebe struggled to free herself, and to my horror, he raised his hand and slapped her face, the crack echoing in the hollow silence. He whispered into her ear, and the phone she'd been holding slipped through her fingers and dropped to the ground. Her attacker pressed his boot on it, sinking it into the feathery snow. Phoebe's eyes rolled back, and I watched as she sank to the ground.

I staggered to my feet. "Help!" I screamed.

The woman threw an iron punch at me, catching my jaw. "I told you to shut it," she hissed. I dropped to the ground at her feet. "One more word and you'll be meeting the same fate as your friend." She kicked Phoebe's unmoving body. "Marcel, do the honours," she added, flourishing her hand toward the man.

I looked on helplessly as Marcel outstretched his arm. All of a sudden, a rupture of shadow lanced through the trees, and my ears started to ring. I gripped my head and cried out in pain.

I could hardly believe what I was seeing. Out of nowhere, the slice of darkness grew until it was the size of Marcel. One moment he was there in front of me, and the next, he stepped through the blackness into nothing. Gone.

The woman hoisted me up by my arm and dragged me into the shadow after Marcel. The last thing I saw as we passed through, was Phoebe's unconscious body left behind in the snow, a trickle of blood spilling from her mouth and leaving a scarlet blemish on the otherwise white world.

I landed down hard on the concrete floor, clipping my skull. The duo stood over me, faces painted in warped exhilaration. Everything around me seemed to spin; the floor, the room, even my attackers. I didn't even get a chance to ground myself before the woman knelt down beside me, her face close to mine.

"Do not speak," she ordered in a throaty voice. "Not a word. Do I make myself clear?"

I kept my mouth clamped shut, staring into her narrowed eyes.

"That's better," she purred. "New blood's learning fast."

She slapped my cheek a couple of times, then stood up and turned to face Marcel. "He told us he'd be here when we arrived. I've got more important things to do than play cat and mouse with this runt." She pointed a slim finger down at me where I lay broken on the hard floor.

"Don't worry," Marcel murmured back. "He'll be here."

I winced, trying to take everything in through my spinning vision. The light was dim in the room, and it seemed like we'd arrived in some abandoned warehouse. Everything was made up of cinder blocks, and graffiti marred the walls. There were windows on one side, some boarded up and some splintered with shattered glass, and there was one door at the far end of the room. No sign of anything I could use as a weapon. Not that I had a chance to get to anything anyway.

My thoughts raced as I tried to piece together who these people were... *What* they were.

A new voice broke the silence. "I see *her* mistake has made it here in one piece. Good work, Amerie."

I flinched at the sound of his voice. How had he gotten so close to me without my noticing? The newcomer was standing over me, his black hair striped with grey and his expression arched into a dark smile. He crouched beside me. An overwhelming presence rolled off him, drowning me into silence.

"Leonard," the woman—Amerie, I assumed—spoke now, "what took you so long? You said you'd be here."

"Now, now Huntress, I was only a few minutes late," Leonard replied, laying a hand on my arm. "Surely you won't condemn me for that?"

Amerie's face pinched into a scowl. "We want our payment."

"Soon," Leonard told her.

"*Now.*"

"You'll receive your payment when *I* say it's time, sister." Leonard spat the last word at her.

They stared at each other for a heated moment, the tension between them palpable.

Then Leonard rumbled with laughter. "My, my. Lilith has her hands full with you, no? Like mother like daughter, I see." Leonard's laugh was deep and echoed across the barren warehouse.

"Then you should know to watch your words with me." Amerie's top lip curled back, and two long canines revealed. Spittle shot across space between them and a fleck hit my cheek.

My pulse quickened.

"You and your drudge can leave now," Leonard replied coolly. "I have what I need, and soon I will deliver your reward." Leonard rose to full high, blocking my view of the duo. There was something about his stance that made me feel like a toy, just an object of possession.

To my surprise, Amerie backed down. "Keep your runts in check, Leo," she said, "otherwise mother will not be so forgiving next time. And you can pass that message on to your darling Collette." There was spite in her voice, hatred.

Leonard glanced at me. "I can assure you that there will not be a *next time*," he muttered.

Instead of replying, Amerie raised her middle finger, and then, the large metal ring enveloping her finger disappeared along with her and Marcel into the melting shadow.

Leonard turned to me slowly. We were alone now. He crouched back down to my level, a sinister smile tugging at his handsome face.

I shivered as he whispered the words, "Welcome to the family."

Chapter Twelve

I awoke to the sound of a voice. Half my face still buried in snow. Cold. Numbingly cold.

His hands were on me.

"Come on," he whispered. "Wake up."

I knew that voice.

It had been a whole year since I'd heard that voice. Twelve months, fifty-two weeks, three-hundred-and-sixty-five days. I wanted to open my eyes to Sam. I wanted to see him, to kiss him… or to kill him, I wasn't sure. All I knew was that I *wanted*.

"Take this," he murmured again. A cold breeze blew onto my face and seeped into my mouth. For a moment I let the feeling sink into me. Suddenly, I was dragged back into consciousness.

"Sam," I wanted to call out to him—to *scream* out to him—but my voice wasn't working. Nothing was working, I was frozen, sinking into the snow.

"Just a little more," the husky voice murmured again. "Come on, Pheebs," he said. "Come back to me."

I felt my chest burn. It was Sam. It was his voice, his words, his touch. His arms were around me; his hands were on me, his whispers were in my ear. He was Sam again, and he was here.

I was caught somewhere between consciousness and delirium, slipping into memory as I tried to grapple for an anchor.

The image of the last time I'd seen Sam, a year ago, played out in my mind like a movie, the screen flickering in and out as my brain fought to awaken. I saw myself holding a blade to his throat. He was breathing fast; shallow, ragged breaths as his golden eyes locked with mine.

"Go on," he seethed. "Do it. I'm begging you. Do it, Phoebe."

His jaw tensed, teeth bared, he wanted me to do it. He wanted me to end it for him. I should have. I should have pressed that blade into his throat, just a little harder, and it would all be over. He'd be over.

But I couldn't. I was weak.

"Breathe in." Sam spoke now, more cool air brushing over my face."Breathe."

On his final word, my eyes shot open, and I drew in an urgent breath. My heart skipped, and for a fraction of a second, he was there, in my mind, or real, I don't know, but I saw him.

And then he was gone. And I was alone beneath the snow-covered trees surrounding the campus.

Alone.

I ran along the stone walkway, dodging the patches of ice that were pooled on the ground. My heart was beating fast.

What the hell just happened?

I could feel the bruise spreading a dull ache across my cheekbone. Vampires. I'd seen it in their blood-red eyes. They'd come for Stef. And I'd let myself get blindsided. I guess it's true what they say; you stop thinking clearly when it gets personal.

And then Sam. I could still feel his breath moving inside of me, reviving me, intoxicating me.

No. I clenched my teeth as I closed in on the entrance to Dorm Block D. I couldn't lose focus—not again.

Although there were a couple of lights illuminating windows inside the dorm building, it was too cold for anyone to be hanging around outside. Fortunately for me, anyway. I'd prefer to dodge any questioning from strangers raising eyebrows at the beat-up, breathless girl running through the snow.

I flung open the main door and raced up the stairwell to the fourth floor. By the time I reached my room, I was trembling, partly from the sprint, but mostly because I was seconds away from losing my head over all of this.

Back inside my dorm room, I pushed the door closed and immediately began rooting through my desk drawers for the standard paper map that had been handed out on our induction day at the start of the semester.

Freeing the map from beneath my notebook, I opened it out and spread it across the floor. Before me, a green and grey lined maze of Briarwood wound around the A1 paper. I'd circled the campus in red, acres of a green band marking my confines.

With a slow breath, I raised my palms over the map. I allowed my eyes to close and my mind to shift to a different wavelength. A familiar heat moved through my chest, enveloping my ribcage. My palms began to tingle, and, slowly, I opened my eyes.

Now, a pale light was weaving gently around my fingers, Guardian energy unveiling itself.

"Find Stefan," I whispered.

A bolt of white light shot from my hands and struck like an arrow, piercing the line that signified the border of Briarwood. A mixture of colours sparked off the page, red, black, gold… And Guardian energy? There was Guardian energy there too?

My heart skipped a beat when I stared down at the location, where embers of iridescent light now fizzled away into nothing, leaving a tiny scorch mark to remind me that they were there.

I knew exactly where the light was leading me.

I just wasn't expecting the *vampires* to be leading me there.

I raced towards the parking lot, scanning the few remaining cars for my Chevy. The truck was in the far corner, where I'd left it just hours earlier. Already there was a dusting of snow on the bonnet, and the wheels were sunken into the white ground.

I flung open the driver's door and slid into my seat behind the steering wheel.

The warehouse? I still couldn't' get my head around it. The vampires took Stef to the warehouse? And there was a Guardian there too?

But that was impossible. A knot formed in my stomach. *I* was the only Guardian who knew about the warehouse.

An echo of Sam played out in my mind. A memory from a long time ago, from the very start, when I'd barely even taken my first step on the firestorm road I was destined to travel with him.

"I found this place," he said, his amber eyes glowing in the dull moonlight dancing on Maura's grave. "I'm going to take it."

"Oh, yeah? What, like an apartment?" Up until then, Sam had been hiding out in the mausoleum in the Briarwood cemetery, where we spent our Saturdays together. He never talked much about his past—the life he'd led before he was turned—but he was alone when he came to Briarwood, and he had been alone for some time since. Before me, that is.

Sam shook his head, dark brown waves curling onto his brow. "Way better than an apartment, Pheebs. It's an abandoned warehouse, right on the outskirts of town. Off Route Six."

I wrinkled my nose. "But that whole area is just marshland. No building can stand there."

"I've seen it," he said, grinning. "I've been there." His hand folded around mine, and he gave my fingers a quick squeeze. "It's a little way off the back roads. I'll show you. It's completely empty. I think it was used for storing iron."

I couldn't help but feel a little excited for him. His enthusiasm was infectious.

"There are thirty rooms," he went on, "maybe more. All empty. I'm going to make it my palace." The corner of his mouth lifted in that sexy way that it did—almost a smile, but more of a smirk.

"And you think you can live there?" I asked. "Won't it be cold."

"I don't get cold," he reminded me. Then added, "But I can put a fireplace in, so you'll be warm."

I allowed myself to imagine, to dream. To picture a world where this reality could be *mine*.

"Come," he said. "Come with me. It'll be ours. You and me, together."

I grinned. "Sounds like you've got it all figured out, Sam."

He planted the smallest of kisses on my lips. "I have," he murmured. "It's going to be a life. Our life, Pheebs."

So, we went to the warehouse that night. With our hands linked, we ran dizzily through the endless cinderblock rooms, dank and cold, but *ours*. That night, as we kissed, fleetingly but urgently, lust flooding through both of us in the most dangerous way, it was our palace. It was our kingdom.

Now, as I drove back there for the first time in a long while, I wasn't going to my kingdom anymore.

Maybe I should have called for back-up. It was dumb to head into the fray alone. Or maybe the Guardians were already there. Either way, I couldn't risk letting them know what I knew.

I couldn't let them storm the palace, for fear that they would kill Sam.

Chapter Thirteen

I found it difficult to place an age on Leonard. Apart from his greying hair and the scruff of a beard that shadowed his jaw, his appearance was strangely youthful. It was only his eyes that held a strange agedness. His stare was striking, both dark and light at the same time, with spirals of golden-brown surrounding the pupils.

"Where am I?" I croaked, my voice shaking. I could hear myself echoing of the warehouse walls. I sounded like a scared child. Even I could hear the fear in the question. Despite my spinning head, I forced myself to sit upright and meet his gaze.

"Nowhere of importance," Leonard replied, his words rebounding in the cavernous warehouse. "We are in a place where the outsiders cannot find us. That's all you need to know, for now." He smiled, flashing his teeth at me.

"Are you going to kill me?" I asked. Saying those words out made my stomach heave with nausea. A cold sweat coated my forehead, and my hands began to shake.

Welcome to the family? That's what Leonard had said to me. They were *not* my family.

"Alas," Leonard replied, "it's too late to kill you." He picked at his teeth with his fingernail and arched a fine eyebrow. "I expected you would have some questions regarding all of this." He gestured to the space around us. "I can assure you that I will get to them. All in due course." He clapped his hands together, and the sound vibrated across the barren room. A tremor moved through the flooring, and then a girl—*the girl*—stepped through the fogged air before us. My blood ran cold.

"You've met my child before, I see…" Leonard said, folding his long arm around her shoulders.

The frail-looking girl who had haunted my life for the past few days stared back at me now with the same eerie golden eyes as Leonard, and raven-black hair hanging limping over her vacant expression.

Child? There was no way Leonard was old enough to be her father. If anything, she looked older then him. I stared numbly back at them, unable to form any words.

"Hello," she murmured to me. Her voice was light, and gone were the grave undertones that had coloured her words the night I'd first seen her. "I need you," was all she said, as real and as tangible as the hard floor beneath me.

Leonard back-handed her across the face, and she dropped to her knees.

I drew in a sharp breath.

"Pathetic," Leonard spat at the girl. "I am ashamed that I ever chose you. You're weak."

She looked up at him from where she cowered, her small face mirroring my horror. A red mark emerged on her porcelain cheekbone, and her black tresses tumbled over it as she bowed her head away from both of us.

Leonard returned his attention to me and his scowl melted into a smile. "I must apologise for my sweet Collette," he said fluidly. "She's new, and she struggles to follow even the simplest of orders. In fact, if she had been wise enough to obey my instructions last week, then you, my friend, would not be here. So, you can thank her for that." His eyes were glowing, like molten lava.

"What are you?" I asked, biting my lip to still the urge to scream.

He only laughed. The sound was so loud that I clapped my hands over my ears. Collette, however, was unaffected by the noise. She clambered to her feet and stood at his side, her head still bowed.

"Monsters, demons, creatures of darkness," Leonard went on. "We have many names. Names that you will soon become familiar with if you survive the turning. I think I'll let Collette explain since she is your sire." He bent down before me, and I gagged at the ashy scent that rolled off him.

"Please, don't kill me!" I cried.

"No no no," Leonard was so close now. His breath smelt of mint, with an undertone of something unpleasant. I couldn't place it. "You are very special my boy, very special indeed." I tried not to listen to his songful voice. I felt his words as if they were trying to lull

83

me into sleep. Suddenly, I snapped out of it, and Leonard was standing away from me again.

"It was a pleasure meeting you, Stefan. I hope that the next time I see you, your heart will still be beating." He looked to Collette, "I trust that you will keep own new member alive and show him kindness as I have shown you."

Collette cowered away but nodded.

Leonard walked up to her and patted her head. "Just as I thought."

Turning back to me a final time he waved, a smile so wide his white teeth seemed to glow. "I am going to have a lot of fun with you, boy."

With a cracking sound, he was gone, dissipated into the shadows of the room. I choked out a breath. He had just evaporated into thin air. He vanished, just inches from my face, as though he had never been there at all; as though he were just a trick of my delirious state.

My focus went to Collette. She wouldn't look back at me.

I knew at that moment that if I wanted to leave, now was my chance.

I jumped to my feet and sprinted across the room. My knees were sore, and my face throbbing from Amerie hit. I didn't look back to see if Collette was following, I just ran. Glass cracked under my sneakers as I trampled over broken shards. I reached the iron door and rattled the handle, but it was locked.

"Please," Collette whispered from across the room. "Please don't run."

I blocked out the sound of her voice as I scrambled for the nearest window, one with a shattered pane. I kicked at the few remaining fractures of glass that clung to the frame and lifted myself through the gap. Shards nipped at my palms as I heaved myself up, but I pushed back the pain and jumped down into the overgrown marshland below.

"There's no point in running." Collette was suddenly standing before me in the tall weeds. "There's nothing around for miles." I stopped in my tracks, turning frantically in a different direction. Turning away from her, I set off again, sprinting through the boggy marsh and fighting my way through the overgrown nature that swamped the warehouse. My heart was pounding so fast and cold air seared as it siphoned into my lungs. I rounded the corner of the derelict building and stopped again. Collette was already on the other side, waiting for me, black hair billowing in the breeze.

"Let me go!" I rasped. "You can't keep me here."

"Please calm down, Stefan," she said softly. "Please listen to me. It'll be worse for you if you run."

I grimaced and turned towards the infringing warehouse. *If I could just find a road*, I thought, I'd wave down a car for help.

"Even if you do get out," Collette went on, "do you believe Leonard won't come after you again? Trust me; you don't want that."

"Why are you doing this to me?" It was more of a plea than a question.

She shuddered. "I couldn't control it. I never meant to leave you alive; I should have killed you." Her lips turned purple from the cold, breath escaping in mist.

"You're not making sense!" I yelled, knotting my fingers through my hair. "None of this makes sense!"

"I was supposed to kill you…" Her words were detached; empty of emotion.

"But I don't even know you," I shouted, and my voice bounced across the run-down building. "Why would you want to kill me? I've never…" I raked my hands through my hair. "*Why*?"

"You don't understand."

"No, I don't!" I exclaimed. "So, tell me! Tell me what I've done to make you do this to me!"

"A few days," she murmured. "That's all you have left." She fixed her gaze on me, her eyes turning almost amber in the slanted light.

"A few days?" I echoed. "What does that mean?"

She opened her mouth to respond, but before she could respond, she flew backwards. Like a rag-doll, her body slammed into the brick wall of the warehouse, and she slumped to the ground.

"Stef!"

I spun around to see Phoebe running towards me. Her arm raised, her palm directed at Collette, who lay groaning on the ground, and the air seemed to ripple in iridescent waves between them.

I looked back at Collette one final time before sprinting towards Phoebe.

"Are you okay?" I asked, pulling her into a hug.

She nodded, breathless. "I'm fine. But we need to get out of here, *now*. There's a road up ahead." She gestured behind her.

"She said she meant to kill me," I huffed as I chased behind Phoebe who led the way through the tall reeds as we fumbled our way towards the road and distant treetops marking the start of a woodland.

"How did you find me?" I yelled as we sprinted for the trees. My jeans were already soaked to the knee from the muddy ground, weighed down by the murky ice water.

"Educated guess," Phoebe called back. "Was there a guardian with you?"

I sprinted next to her, almost falling at her question.

"A what?" I panted, scared to turn around and see Collette chasing.

Phoebe didn't answer me, and I didn't care. I wanted to get as far away from this place as possible.

We reached a chain link fence, cordoning the warehouse and marshland from the road. The crisscross wires had been cut open, and we slipped through the gap. The moment I left the boundaries of the warehouse; relief overcame me.

Ahead, Phoebe's Chevy truck was parked on the gravel road

"Buckle up!" Phoebe shouted as she flung open the driver's door.

I clambered into the passenger's seat and stared out of the rear window as Phoebe pressed her foot down on the accelerator and we swerved out onto the road. Through the back window, I watched Collette stand in the middle of the road, between our tyre tracks, her black hair stirring in the breeze. I watched until she was nothing more than a dot in the distance.

Chapter Fourteen

I paced around Phoebe's family's living room, ignoring the concerned glances from May, Michael, and Phoebe as they sat together on the sofa. Their intense stares bore down on me. I was full of anxiety after what had happened I almost burst.

What I'd gathered from mine and Phoebe's hell-for-leather drive across town, was that the warehouse was part of some abandoned factory that occupied the barren space on the borders of Briarwood. I'd never heard of the factory before, but it would not be a place I'd be forgetting anytime soon.

"You are ten steps away from wearing a hole in the rug," May remarked from the sofa. "I wouldn't mind, but that Persian belonged to my grandmother." She offered me a shrewd smile.

I stopped, hands clenched at my sides. "Can someone please just tell me what the hell is going on?"

I didn't miss May's recoil from my curt tone. I didn't mean for my words to bite out like that, but I needed answers. *Now.*

"The girl from my dream is real," I said in a ragged breath. "There people—these *things*—evaporate into thin air. And you," I turned my gaze upon Phoebe. "I saw something… When you faced the girl, Collette, I saw something change the air between you. It…*rippled.*"

Phoebe stared down at her fingernails. "I would have told you. I wanted to tell you…"

"Tell me *what?*" I yelled.

Michael cleared his throat, and May let out a slow breath.

When Phoebe looked up at me, her jade eyes were glassy.

"Come on, Phoebe," I whispered.

She stayed silent.

Suddenly Michael rose to his feet. "I can explain," he said, his voice strange and hollow. "There's more to this world than what meets the eye. There is an entire world of our own that most people simply do not know about."

"The underworld," Phoebe filled in, quietly.

"Yes," Michael went on. "An underworld of beings that most humans will never have the displeasure of meeting. Unfortunately, you have met them, Stef. And despite our best efforts, it seems you will continue to meet them." He gestured towards Phoebe's mum, and said, "May foresaw your fate in the runes, and when we spoke with you at the house earlier, it only confirmed what we already believed."

I was listening, but it was near-impossible to make any sense of what Michael was telling me. "Those people," I stammered. "The ones who jumped me, they're part of the underworld?"

"Demons," Phoebe answered. "Children of Lilith."

A week ago, I might have laughed at a statement like that. I *would* have laughed. But after what I'd seen today, demons didn't seem so unbelievable.

And that name, I suddenly remembered. *Lilith*. That's the name Leonard had used when he was talking to Amerie. He'd said, *Lilith has her hands full with you. Like mother like daughter.*

"So, they're demons," I said, swallowing. "These *Children of Lilith*, as you called them. And now they're, coming after me?"

May inhaled slowly. "I wish it were that simple…"

I noticed Phoebe chewing her thumbnail. She wouldn't meet my eyes.

"Elaborate," I said, my voice flat.

And May did. "We believe that your visit from the girl has proven to be detrimental to you. We believe that she was turning—transitioning from human to demon—and was required to take a soul that night, to take a life. But she failed with you when she didn't complete the sacrifice. She left you in limbo, suspended between life and death."

My mouth fell open as I groped for words. "But, I'm alive," I said, dazed.

"Yes," May's voice was calm and even. "And now Leonard wants to find you. He wants to recruit you."

Leonard? How did she know his name? I was certain I hadn't mentioned it.

"You know him?" I asked, hoarsely. "You know Leonard?"

"Yes. Unfortunately, we do."

Chapter Fifteen

I saw Stef's face when my mother broke the news about Leonard. I saw that scared and helpless look as May served the harsh reality. Stef was as good as dead, even if mum hadn't directly said so.

Mum had warned me though. She'd warned me about what could happen to innocent people if we didn't do our job properly. It was a little over a year ago, during my senior year at high school, and the semester had barely begun when mum had first confronted me about Sam. For two whole years I'd been meeting with Sam in secret, and in all that time my mum had said nothing. I'd been dumb enough to assume that was because she didn't know, that I'd somehow kept this under her radar.

But when she'd finally confronted me, I guess that was the moment I realised that my mother knew *everything*.

Well, not everything, exactly.

There was still one thing she didn't know.

"Apparently I'm supposed to start applying to colleges. Can you believe that?" I laughed as I looked up at the half moon in the ebony sky, my head lolling back onto the gravestone and my fingers laced through Sam's. It was balmy that night, still hot from the Indian summer we'd had in Briarwood. "Senior year has hardly begun, and already everyone's preparing for next year. Crazy, right?"

"Yeah," Sam murmured.

"Anyway," I went on, tugging at the blades of grass growing over Maura's grave, "if I *do* have to apply to schools, I'm thinking of majoring in Bio-Chemistry."

When Sam didn't respond, I turned to him. His eyes were almost closed.

"What do you think?" I prompted. "Do you think Bio-Chemistry would be good?"

"Sounds hard," he answered without looking at me.

"Well, yeah. But it's interesting, the science of our cells and molecular structure. Of all people, that should interest us."

He flinched.

"Whatever," I said, brushing over his terse reaction. "I think it sounds interesting. I'd like to understand you, and how you..." I let the sentence taper off. *Changed.* That's what I'd wanted to say. And could he blame me? I wanted to study the science that explained how a once normal boy could change into an Incubus demon by the act of cell transmutation.

"It doesn't interest me," he said as if he were reading my thoughts. "I don't care. We are what we are."

We are what we are?

He was staring off at the constellations in the night sky. His mind was with the stars, not me. But this distance between us wasn't entirely unfamiliar. He'd been distant for a while. Three weeks, maybe more. It made my stomach knot.

I squeezed his fingers. "Where are you?"

He turned to me, catching my gaze and smiling carefully. "I'm right here, Pheebs."

"Physically," I said, arching an eyebrow. "But where's your mind?"

He sighed and rubbed his brow. "I don't know," he murmured. "It's a lot, isn't it? I mean, Phoebe, what do you expect me to say? You're planning on going off to college. I'm not there. And I never will be."

Oh.

"It's just a thought," I said. "I'm probably not going to college, anyway. I'm not *there*, either."

"You could be." His jaw clenched. "You *should* be."

"You know that's not how I see my life," I snorted at the idea. "I mean, me? College?" Okay, so there'd been a fleeting moment where I'd envisaged myself pacing quickly through a brownstone campus with a harassed look upon my face as I strode between classes, lugging around heavy science textbooks, but really... it was all just fantasy.

"Why not?" Sam's tone was serious, his shadowed eyes never leaving mine. "Why wouldn't you go to college?"

"Many reasons," I said. I shifted on the earth, letting my fingers slip from his.

"Such as?"

"My grades aren't good enough," I said; it was the truth. Balancing guardian training and school was hard. It was showing in my grade reports just how much effect it was having on me. "I have responsibilities here."

"Like what?"

"This," I said, patting the grass on the grave. "I'm a Guardian. And I've been responsible for this Saturday night shift for two years—"

"So? Your mum can take over."

I sighed. "Sam…"

"Give me a better reason than that."

"Fine," I said. "You." There. That's what he'd been leading to, we both knew it.

He grimaced. "Exactly. I'm holding you back."

"Only on Saturday nights," I said with a quick smile.

"It's more than Saturday night's though, isn't it? It's life, mortality. All of which I have none of, and you have in abundance. It's laying out before you, waiting for you to seize it."

"I'm already seizing it," I said. My chest tightened. I didn't like where this was going. And it wasn't the first time we'd been here.

"Maybe," he said.

"My life is just fine," I told him. "We'll make it work. I have you; you have me. I'm not going anywhere." Even as I spoke the words, I felt something tug in my subconscious.

A gust of wind dragged through the trees in the cemetery, rustling their leaves as though they were laughing at me; laughing at *us*.

"Things are changing," he went on, his tone altering, shifting in a way that I didn't understand, his golden eyes glinting in a way that I didn't recognise. "But there are options, Phoebe. There are options that we haven't even considered yet."

I stiffened. "Such as?"

He blew out a breath. "Maybe you need to meet with Leonard, and…"

Leonard. The name alone made my gut twist. Ever since the mysterious Incubus demon, Leonard, had shown up in Briarwood a few months ago, Sam had been acting differently. He was part of some weird community now, where this Leonard promised something to the undead. A life without meaning. But in my opinion, Leonard sounded like a creep, a cult leader that lost souls gravitated towards. Of course, I didn't like the thought of Sam being alone, but I didn't like the thought of him being headhunted by this Leonard guy, either.

"…and he already knows all about you—"

"Whoa." I raised my hand, cutting him off. "You talk to Leonard about me?"

"Well, yeah," Sam looked at the ground, then back up again. "I have to talk to someone, Pheebs. I'm going out of my mind; the thought that this could be your last year in Briarwood. You keep growing older and moving on to new stages of life, and I'm frozen. Forever stuck in the shadows of my demonic tendencies." He pressed his thumbs against his chest.

Sam. My eyes wandered over him. He was still the same eighteen-year-old boy I'd met two years ago, totally unaltered. The only difference was *me*. I'd caught up with him now, and I'd keep growing, changing, ageing...

"You tell Leonard all of this?" I asked. A spike of apprehension moved through my veins.

"Yeah. Just about our situation, our lives together. You know, with you being a Guardian and me being an Incubus. He gets it, Pheebs."

"Oh." I bristled. "So, what does he say?"

"He did come up with a solution if you're interested." I saw the hopefulness in Sam's gaze, and I felt sick all of a sudden, almost as if my body knew what was coming before my brain did.

Then his words spilt out into the quiet night, "What if I turned you?"

I stared back at him, silently.

He rubbed his knuckles over his mouth, almost as though he'd mistaken my silence for consideration. Like I was sitting there pondering the pros and cons. *Oh sure, turn me into a demon so we can live immortally together, forever.* I adored Sam, I was obsessed with him, addicted, in love with him, even. But I'd never willingly hand myself over; I would never turn into a demon for him.

I swallowed down a sudden pain in my throat.

"How could you even ask that of me?"

Something in the air changed, and I picked up the energy of a vampire nearby.

"Hold on," I whispered to Sam. I sprung to my feet.

"Phoebe…" he said my name.

"I'll be back," I promised him. Frankly, I was glad to have a distraction; I was glad to have an excuse to walk away. My mind was whirling as I numbly trailed the movement through the cemetery, leaving Sam behind at Maura's grave. Tears began to burn down my cheeks.

My sights locked on the vampire prowling amongst the headstones. It was a newbie, I could tell from its hollow eyes and loose-limbed gate. I targeted it, closing in. It swung for me, and I threw a punch harder than I ever had before. Without missing a beat, I drew my stake and plunged it into the creature's chest, harder than ever before, almost as though I was vanquishing *everything*—mortality, immortally, and the cruel fate that had brought Sam and me together, only to kill us off in the end.

To hell with fate.

As the vamp turned to dust with a piercing scream, I let out a rough breath. Tears spill down my cheeks, uncontrollable, soundless.

"Pheebs?"

I turned quickly. Sam was standing behind me, bathed in moonlight. His dark hair stirred in the midnight breeze. He just looked at me, his expression sober, as though he'd realised what I'd realised.

I ran to him, pressed my lips to his and kissed him as though I would never kiss him again.

I knew at that moment that this would be the last time. My mind was made up.

His arms closed around me. "Please," he whispered. "Please forget I said anything. We can keep going, just like this. Please don't leave me, Pheebs."

But it was too late. I was already gone. For both of our sakes, I had to be.

I arrived back home that night just as dawn was beginning to rise over Briarwood. My whole body ached, my eyes swollen, and face damp from crying. The moment I walked through the front door, I was met by my parents.

My mother hugged me. It was a strange feeling. We weren't a 'hugging' family, so I bristle beneath their embrace. Not wanting to feel love or weakness ever again. Suddenly I couldn't breathe, as though the life was squashed from my lungs.

I let out a choked sound.

"Sit down," Mum ordered, guiding me to the living room.

Trembling and fragile, I lowered myself onto the sofa. Dad hovered at a safe distance, while Mum handed me a lavender tea.

"This will calm you," she said.

I wanted to throw the china teacup at the wall. I wanted it to shatter as I had. Into many tiny, unfixable pieces.

Dad watched from afar, I knew he felt my pain, but he had no words for me. That was okay. I had no words, either.

"Poor girl." Mum sat down beside me and folded her hand around mine. "I knew tonight would be the night."

Numbly I processed her words. *Sam*, I realised instantly. She'd known about Sam all along, right up to the point where we would reach our demise. So my mother was privy to my break up with my secret boyfriend? That alone was another steel blade to the abdomen.

"I'm sorry, honey," she whispered. "Truly, I am. I hate seeing you so hurt. But you know this is the way it has to be. It is for the best."

"I know, Mum," I reply through gritted teeth. "That's why I did it."

Dad gave me a pained look. "We're both so sorry that you're going through this."

"It'll get easier." Mum squeezed my fingers.

Right. How would she know? She married her childhood sweetheart.

I tried to nod, or speak, or even just smile, but the expression couldn't form yet.

"Phoebe…" Mum went on. Her tone had shifted, turning businesslike. She was *May* now, the Guardian. "I know this is hard, but we need you to tell us where the lair is…"

The lair?

"They're colonising," she continued. "I've foreseen it. We need to stop them before their numbers get too great."

Suddenly the tick of the grandfather clock seemed deafening loud. Her words sounded jumbled in my ears.

"A new Incubus is forming a colony," she said. "Their leader goes under the name Leonard. We need to take him down before he recruits more."

I stared blearily into my lavender tea, watching the sprigs dance on the murky surface. "I can't," I murmured. "I don't know."

My parents swapped an exasperated look.

"Please, Phoebe," my mother implored. "This isn't a game. We need to act fast. Where is the Incubus hideout? Your friend, the boy, he must have told you."

The words were stinging, rupturing my heart. I was supposed to tell them where Sam lived, so they could go and slay him?

"Mum," I choked out a sob. "Please. I don't know where the lair is," the lie tumbled from my lips, fractured.

"He's killing, Phoebe. They both are. And they'll keep doing it until we stop them."

"Phoebe," Dad spoke softly. "Please."

Phoebe, please. The words stung, and I never wanted to hear them again.

I shook my head. "I don't know."

But that was then. That was the past. Now, Stefan was paying the price, hiding out at our house while we all waited for the inevitable.

I wished I had told my parents where the lair was that night.

The warehouse, I should have said. *It's just outside of Briarwood.*

I wished I'd told them that back then.

And I wished I had the strength to tell them now.

But in my heart, I hoped to spot Sam there. I didn't see him, but I knew he was watching. I'd felt it like cold fingers trailing down my neck.

Chapter Sixteen

Phoebe was already asleep on the single mattress in her childhood bedroom. It didn't take her long to fall asleep, although the timing seemed convenient to me like it was preferable to my incessant questioning. What can I say? I had a lot of questions, and she had a lot of answers.

I lay in the spare bed, staring up at the ceiling. I could hear movement in the room above me—May and Michaels' room—it sounded as if someone were pacing, opening drawers with aged creaks. I lay awake, fighting the hunger pains in my stomach and the wild thoughts tearing through my mind.

Demons. Guardians. Me.

May had explained that Leonard was one of Lilith's children three offspring. *Lilith*, her name echoed in my mind. The mother of demons, child of the fallen, and queen of the underworld. All titles that chilled me to the core. It turned out I had met two of the three in a matter of moments today. Leonard, born of lust. Amerie, a vampire created from Lilith's spilt blood. And the third, an unnamed demon whom the guardians know very little about.

I rolled over and glanced at Phoebe's peaceful face. *Guardian.* All this time, I'd never seen past the veil of what she and her family truly were. Protectors.

And then there was me, the infected. *The dammed,* as Michael had put it. Trapped halfway between life and death.

Collette, Leonard, Amerie, Lilith. These names had meant nothing to me twenty-four hours ago. Now they meant everything.

I watched with intent as the shadows in the room danced. Was it me? I wondered. Were the stirring shadows a result of my affliction? The hunger, the rush of blood in my veins, the shadows.

Answers. That's what I hungered for most. And yet no question I asked seemed to get me to the core of this living nightmare.

May dropped us off at the campus the following morning. It was Friday, and classes were drawing to a close for Christmas break. Since most students had left already; we were only wasting hours watching films in class and finishing up on overdue projects. Already the snow-dusted campus was looking more desolate, fewer cars in the parking lot, fewer people strolling along the walkways.

I grimaced as we passed by the same walkway that had resulted in my run-in with Amerie and Marcel.

Honestly, I wasn't even sure I could face coming back here. But Phoebe and I had one more Bio Chem class before we finished the year, and somehow the distraction of it felt welcomed. My mind was jumbled, and I didn't know why I was going to class, pretending like everything was normal. Well, maybe that was just it. That was what I needed right now, for everything to be normal. So I was willing to pretend.

I don't think Phoebe was in quite the same mindset because she fumbled over a lame excuse about cleaning her dorm room, an excuse to ditch class, or to avoid me, I wasn't sure anymore.

So, alone, I made my way to the main building. As I ascended the concrete steps, I felt the burning existence within me, a poisonous feeling. Something was inside of me now, something alien.

I arrived at Professor Markell's lab a little before class was due to start.

When I opened the door, Professor Markell was at the front of the room, peering down into a microscope.

"Oh!" he looked up with a start. "Stefan. You're early." His snowy eyebrows shot up in surprise.

I summoned a smile. "Yeah, well, I figured I should be early at least once this semester, right?"

He chuckled pleasantly. "It's good to see you. I know this end of semester class can be considered a throwaway to a lot of my students." He slipped on his glasses. "How have you found this as a major? I know you've been absent a few times this year."

I shifted under his gaze. "Yeah, I owe you an apology Professor."

He waved off my apology. "I'm glad you've decided to stick with it. Bio-Chemistry is a fascinating subject, and you show great potential. The last thesis you wrote blew my expectations out of the water."

I drew in a deep breath. "Can I ask you something?" I glanced over my shoulder into the empty lab. I could perpetually feel eyes on me these days. Paranoid? Most definitely.

"Of course." He folded his hands together on the desktop.

"Is it possible to alter the molecular structure of a human?"

"Absolutely," he said. "Genetic mutation has proven that."

"Okay, so what if a person, was infected with blood or salvia, could that change the genetics?"

His brow furrowed.

I elaborated, "If an animal bit me, for example, could part of that animal then transfer into me, affecting my DNA?"

He rubbed the white stubble on his jawline. "If a dog bit you, it would be biologically impossible to transfer part of the dog's genetic makeup into you. However, if a dog bit you with rabies, then you would be infected with the rabies virus."

"So it's the virus," I surmised. Whatever Collette did to me has given me a virus.

"Stefan?" Professor Markell stared fixedly into my eyes. "Is everything okay? You seem a little... *unwell*."

Unwell? Now there was an understatement.

I almost told him. I almost just blurted it out right there and then, like he was a parent and I was a helpless child needing comfort. But the words never reached the surface.

"And a virus can be treated?" I questioned, "Reversed."

Professor Markell made a face, tilting his head like a confused pup. "What do you think would happen if a dog had a bad case of rabies? If it became a threat to others around it?"

"It would be sectioned?" I replied.

He shook his head, "It would be put down."

The change in his tone was sudden. I took a step back, smiling awkwardly as I stumbled to my seat. Professor Markell didn't take his eyes off me until the room began to fill with students.

Chatter began to spread through the room, everyone in high spirits with Christmas holidays around the corner. I was in a daze, though. I just kept my head down and tried my best to focus on the lesson plan.

We were studying ion-exchange, methylene and haemoglobin, and since Phoebe had bailed today, I'd joined a temporary lab partner.

I poured a phial of methylene blue liquid into a tube and lifted a sample of PH7 phosphate. My muscles spasmed as I reached up, almost making me drop the phosphate. The muscle spasms had started this morning. What had once felt like a dull hunger pain, now felt more like a bout of flu, turning my stomach and making my limbs ache. May had assured me that she was working on a tonic to help ease the pain. I could only wonder what that meant.

"A little at a time," my lab partner snapped, prizing the methylene tube from my fingers. He was a thin boy, with blond hair and a narrow, crooked nose. "It's eluted already. Now we have to add the PH 5.5."

"I know," I muttered, watching the blue chemical split from the red in the tube. "I understand the experiment." I selected another phial and raised it.

He snatched the phial before I could tip it. "I'll do it," he grumbled.

"I can do it," I replied, frowning.

"You're doing it wrong." His angular face pulled into a scowl. "How did you even get accepted into this major?"

I bit down on my tongue.

"Must have been a short waiting list," my lab-partner uttered under his breath.

"I've got a lot on my mind," I managed.

He cackled out a laugh. "Maybe you'd be better off in a different class, something a little less complex."

A rush of anger bubbled inside of me. Who did this guy think he was? *The last thing I need is to have to deal with jumped up asshats like*—

Suddenly loud popping sounds started around the room. Beakers exploded in showers of glass and water, and the lab erupted in screams.

I could still feel that same growing presence inside of me, but this time in every inch of my body, from my feet to the tips of my fingers. The burning energy twisted within me. Pain, all I could feel was pain. Burning, hot, stabbing agony that flooded through me.

I staggered out from my workbench and stumbled for the exit, just as the safety sprinklers set off, raining water from the ceiling.

I ran out of the lab and ran down the hall. My vision started to speckle and blur. I slipped into an empty office and the next thing I knew, I was on the floor, fighting the urge to pass out. I saw double, two desks, two cabinets and two sets of windows… My head was spinning.

I reached into my jeans pocket and pulled out my phone. My hands trembled as I tried to focus on the screen, then blearily found Phoebe's number and pressed call.

I gripped it tightly as the dial tone began in my ear.

"Stef?" Phoebe's voice sounded across the line.

"Hey," I choked. "Something happened. The lab…I…"

"Whoa, Stef," her voice was soothing. "Slow down. What happened?"

"I...I don't know. Something's changing, Phoebe. Something's *in* me. I don't understand," I groped for words. "I don't understand what happened to me that night, with the girl. With Collette." Saying her name aloud sent shockwaves through my system.

"Stef..." Phoebe's voice returned to me.

"Please," I begged her, staring up at the window, where snow had caught in the edges of the pane. "Please just tell me what happened? Tell me what they've done to me? Trapped between life and death, but what does that mean? I'm changing, Phoebe. I know I am."

"Stef, you're dying."

The words hit me like a tidal wave.

"Stef, I'm sorry," Phoebe was crying on the phone. "I didn't want to keep this from you. Mum and dad told me it would be easier if you didn't know, and to just carry on like everything was normal but..."

"I'm dying?" I breathed.

"You've been infected. We can't reverse it."

Professor Markless words flooded back to me.

My fingers fastened tighter around the phone. "How long?"

"A few days." I could hear her shattered breaths. "I ... I wanted to tell you. You have to believe me."

"A few days?" I echoed numbly.

"Four. Maybe five."

I wanted to laugh, to accuse her some sick practical joke, but the words died on my tongue.

I forced myself to sit upright. "Phoebe," my voice was stronger than it had been a moment ago. Stronger than it had been for days. "This can't be it. There has to be another way…"

There was silence on her end of the phone.

"I have to go," I said hoarsely.

"Stef," she cried, "where are you going? Tell me where you are, I'll find you. We can talk about this."

I didn't answer. I wouldn't.

There was one place I was certain to get answers. Collette.

I picked myself from the floor, ran down the corridor and left the building without a glance behind me.

I didn't stop running until I saw the warehouse in my view.

CHAPTER SEVENTEEN

"Hello...?" I called.

My voice echoed across the barren warehouse, loud and distant. Each time I called out, I stilled my breathing, listening for any signs of movement. I gritted my teeth when a rat scurried out from beneath a pile of crates and shot across the floor into the shadows.

I placed my hand on my heart, feeling the uncomfortable beat. Aimlessly, I forged on through endless rooms with their graffiti-covered walls and burlap sacks and rubble. I was so far into the maze of the warehouse that I didn't think I could find my way out again, even if I'd wanted to.

"Collette..." Saying her name aloud was still strange. Only yesterday her presence had terrified me, but she seemed to be the only one willing to talk. Everyone else, Phoebe and the so-called Guardians, were happier to keep me in the dark. And hell, I was a monster now, right? Maybe the dark was where I belonged.

In fact, it was the growing darkness within me that drove me forward. It was as though I was being pulled now, drawn into the room after room until I noticed a burning light spill beneath a door frame.

Time seemed to slow down for a moment. She was there, through that door, and she was waiting for me. I could feel it. There was a tug on my chest, a pull that I couldn't explain, urging me forward. Guiding me to her. I gave into it and walked, pushing the door wide to see Collette seated in a leather chair by a smouldering log fire.

"You came back," she murmured. Her voice was soft for a demon. She turned to look at me, a look of sadness plastered across her face.

She faced me, and her golden gaze sent shockwaves over my skin.

"What have you done to me?" It was all I could say. I pushed my fear down and held her stare. "You've *changed* me."

"Sit down," she whispered. "And I will tell you everything you need to know."

I moved over to her, taking a seat on a worn down stool. It almost felt like she was waiting for me.

"Why me?" I demanded.

She exhaled softly. "I followed you," she said simply "For a long time, I followed you." Everything about her seemed to glow with the pulse of the fire, angelic and demonic all at once.

"What do you mean, you followed me?"

"I chose you. I didn't have long to make a choice."

"But why?" I pressed, my voice shaking.

"I don't know," she breathed. "I existed in a state of pure lust and greed. An ever-burning hunger for souls. When I saw you, I felt a lost boy. Even with your friends, you seemed to be distant. In a warped way, I thought I would be doing you a favour by taking your soul."

I grimaced.

"But you didn't kill me?"

She shook her head, "I couldn't. As I breathed your soul, I was memories. It shocked me, the sudden wave of love that greeted my lips. In a split moment, I knew I couldn't do it to you."

"The told me I'm dying…" I said, staring into the fire. I felt oddly comfortable around her, even after the things she had admitted.

"The Guardians, you mean?" She asked, her tone becoming inquisitive now. "You came back here on your own accord because they are keeping you in the dark."

"I had to," I choked out the words, balling my hands into fists as I spoke. "I had to know more. I had to know what you were trying to tell me before I…" I let the sentence trail off. "I don't want to die."

Her eyes darkened. "Well, Leonard has made sure your Guardian friend won't get that close to us again. He has eyes in places even I have still not worked out."

Phoebe. I shivered. "Did you know I was coming?" I asked.

"I had hoped."

I looked at her; *really* looked. She was striking. There was something otherworldly about her expression

117

something haunting. Compared to when I first saw her, she had filled out. Her flesh pulsed with colour and life.

She gave a musical laugh. "The guardians will want you to believe you are dying. That is what they want you to believe. They would rather you not survive the transition; it means you will be one less demon to kill in the long run. The Guardians want nothing more than for all of us just to disappear."

"I can survive this?" I croaked.

She nodded; silently.

"Then tell me, you must tell me how to fix this."

She looked down to the fire, the red flames reflecting her golden eyes.

"Please…" I begged.

The realisation of betrayal blurred the promise of survival.

My own friend and her family, who I believed to be close to my own, wanted me dead. They kept this from me.

"Sometimes, the answers you seek are not the ones you wish to hear."

"Just tell me," I said, sitting up straight.

She opened her arms wide. "You simply allow yourself to become one of us. It happened to me, too. And that's how I…that's why I did what I did to you. I did it to survive."

I stared at her, bristling as her admission sank in. She did this to me to survive?

"A few months ago," she carried on, "I was just a normal girl." Her gaze became almost wistful, drifting around the windowless room. "I was just a girl who got caught up with the wrong crowd. When I came to your room that night, I was on the last day of my transition, and the pain of death was unbearable. Leonard, my creator, told me what I had to do to survive, but I refused. A soul for a soul, that's what Leonard said."

"A soul for a soul," I echoed back.

"I didn't want my survival to be at the cost of another's life, but I couldn't go through the pain anymore, I knew I had to do it. So I came to you."

"Why?" I asked hoarsely. "Why me?"

She licked her lips, her eyes darting away from me anxiously. "As I said, I followed you. I'd been following you."

The air in the room prickled my skin.

"For how long?" I pressed.

"A while. I was drawn to you, and I couldn't resist anymore. But when I began the Death kiss, I panicked." She tugged at a strand of her long hair, suddenly appearing child-like under my condemning stare. "It was as though, in that final moment, I came to my senses. I was afraid, and I felt ashamed, guilty. I didn't want to murder you to satisfy my hunger, my own selfish damned life. So I stopped."

"But it was too late," I filled in the blanks.

"I thought I'd spared you," she said. "But I didn't realise I'd left you in limbo."

My breath faltered. "Between life and death," I managed.

She nodded. "Leonard was angry. He wanted to be the only sire because a sire has the control and the power. So he brought me back to finish the job. But I refused to take him to you. I couldn't do it. So, I lied. I took him to the wrong room, and he made me complete the transition."

I couldn't take my eyes of Collette, and I knew my mouth was wide open. I could see the sadness in her eyes as she spoke, but I felt no sympathy for her.

"Jeanie," I said. "You killed her. *I* was supposed to die that night, but you took Jeanie's life instead."

She bowed her head. "I suppose not all of us are cut out for this. I've thought about that girl's face every day since. I dream about her." She squeezed her eyes shut, then exhaled in a long breath. "I can't put right what I've done, but I can't let her death be in vain."

My eyebrows drew together. "In vain? You *killed* her," I spat. "You murdered her. And you tried to murder me!"

She shook her head, hair tumbling around her shoulders. "No," she said empathically. "Not yet. You don't have to die. You can live. All you have to do is make a kill, just like I did—"

I staggered back from her. "Are you insane?"

"I'm Leonard's child," she whispered. "Leonard sired me, and now I'm just like him. I know you think I'm a monster, and perhaps I am. But during the transition, I lost all control. You'll feel it, too. Each day will get worse. The hunger becomes unbearable, and soon, you either take a life or die at the mercy of the affliction."

I wanted to leave, I wanted to run, but I was frozen, my gaze lost in the burning flames. I clenched my fists, my fingernails cutting half-moon shapes into the palms of my hands.

"You are part of our world now," Collette murmured. "And we'll take care of you."

"What are you, Collette?" I already knew the answer. For she was Leonard's child.

Her shoulders shook as she laughed. I tilted my head, confused by the reaction. Nothing about this seemed funny to me.

"You're lucky," she said, taking a breath. "You're lucky that Amerie has nothing to do with what you are."

I thought back to when I'd met Amerie, and the pointed teeth she'd displayed when she growled at Leonard.

"She's a vampire?" I asked. "Amerie's a vampire?"

"Correct. Vampires are a product of Amerie. As for me—*us*, that is, *we* are different. I'm a Succubus, a manifestation of dark passion. Leonard is an Incubus. The male counterpart."

My heart rate quickened. "And that means that I'm also an Incubus?"

"Not yet," she replied. "But you could be."

"Why would I want that?" I shouted into the quiet room. "Why would I *ever* choose that?"

"Because it's better than the alternative," she answered calmly. "It's better than death."

The fire's flames leapt higher on her final word, and my blood ran cold.

"Just wait," she went on. "In a few days, you must decide whether you will exist in your new form, or die with the old."

I dug my nails deeper into my palms. "You're telling me, that if I want to survive, I…"

"You must take a life," she finished the sentence for me. "And replenish your wilting body with the soul of another."

Chapter Eighteen

I reclined on my bed in my room at my parents' house, watching through the sash window as the sun cast amber beams across the backyard. Frost clung to the rose bushes; their thorns turned white in winter's grasp.

My door didn't creak open, but someone stepped into the room with me.

"Back again," I said, without turning around. "Didn't you learn the last time?"

"I was wrong," Jeanie replied, sounding withered. "I shouldn't have treated you like that."

I sat upright and turned to look at her. Jeanie, her translucent face *there*, but somewhere else as well. She was still in her ghostly form, and apparently, she'd managed to leave the confines of Dorm Block D. Damn it. I'd sort of hoped she would have headed into the light by now. I wasn't in the mood to counsel spirits with unfinished business.

"Stef has gone to the warehouse," she said, tapping her weightless foot on the bedroom floorboards. "That place where those things are hiding out. You know that, right?"

I sighed, my eyes trained on her through the dim lamplight. "Yes, I know," I said. I'd figured as much.

"So?" Jeanie extended her hands, as if to say, *get a move on, your friend is in trouble, you idiot!* But it was too late to *get a move on.* Stef may have only just arrived at the warehouse, but it was still *days* too late for intervention.

"There's nothing I can do right now," I said, hearing the apathy in my voice. "This is Stef's choice, not mine."

Jeanie pursed her lips. "Stef's choice? So you're just going to let another innocent person die?"

I winced. Jeanie's words plunged into my ribcage, piercing my heart. "It's too late," I muttered. "The damage is already done for Stef. For both of you. You should move on, let go of this anger and move to the other side." I was *days* too late.

There was a beat of silence between us, and then she spoke again.

"Oh, *now* I get it." She gave a throaty chuckle.

I raised my eyebrows. "Care to elaborate?"

"You *want* Stef to be at the warehouse. Better to be one of them and kill a couple of innocents than be dead, right?"

I sucked in a sharp breath. "No," I cried. "No, that's not it at all! Of course, I want Stef to survive, and I wish that could be possible. But I'm a Guardian; my vocation is to protect innocents from demons— Not help demons move past the transition."

She simpered. "Keep telling yourself that."

Did she know about Sam? The thought made my stomach flip with guilt.

Jeanie folded her arms, and I noticed the faint outline of my dresser visible through her foggy torso. "Aren't you even going to *try* to avenge me?" she asked. "As you say, you're a demon hunter, aren't you? Shouldn't you be out there, killing demons?"

Uck. The undead can be so self-righteous. "I'm trying my best," I said, sitting up a little straighter. "My job isn't easy, you know. But I'm trying."

"Oh, really?" she scoffed. "Because it looks like you're hanging out at your mum's house wallowing in self-pity."

I frowned at her. She'd been omniscience for, like, a minute, and suddenly she's the freaking oracle celestial being that needs instant avenging?

But I'd already been to the warehouse once. I'd charged in to rescue Stef the first time, and it had worked. For a second, at least. And now? Well, I guess the demon pull was too strong for Stef to resist now. I wasn't going back there again; it was painful enough to go back once, let alone on a second fool's mission.

Yesterday hadn't been my first ambush on the warehouse. I'd been a year ago, when Leonard had first started turning innocents, forming an army, and that trip hadn't worked out too well either.

I'd gone there to kill him. *Sam*, I mean. But I couldn't get the blade to pierce the skin; my hands refused to obey me.

125

"Go on," his words echoed in my memory, "do it. I'm begging you. Do it, Phoebe."

But I let him go. I fled from the place, leaving Leonard and Sam unharmed, and free to turn as many victims as they chose.

And now Jeanie was dead, Stef was as good as dead—or worse, a demon.

But at least Sam was still alive, hey?

And maybe, for him, that was worse.

"Do you know why the demons are crowding in Briarwood?" Jeanie sang, "Do you?"

I stared at her, "No, but I am sure you're going to tell me."

"How about you help Stefan, and as a reward, I will tell you everything I have overheard." She turned as if to walk through my bedroom wall, "But be quick. A storm is brewing in this town. Don't wait until it devours you all."

CHAPTER NINETEEN

Collette tilted her head; her ear angled to the door as if she were listening to something beyond the four barren walls of the fire-lit room in the warehouse.

"Leonard," she whispered.

The word alone could have turned my body to ice. Collette's serene face crumpled in fear.

I looked at the door—the exit that was my only escape route.

"No," Collette called to me, raising her hand. "Don't run. He knows you're here."

The sound of heavy footsteps echoed, growing louder as Leonard neared the room. Collette busied herself with feeding the dwindling fire with logs, but my eyes didn't leave the door as I waited for it to open, waited for him to appear.

An entire world had unveiled for me, and through my foggy mind, I could barely make sense of any of it. All I knew was that Leonard was someone to fear. *Something* to fear.

I held my breath as he stepped around the door frame, dressed in a worn leather jacket and ripped jeans. At a glance, he could have been just another college kid on campus. But something about him was older, stronger. Something about him was inhuman. And now I knew why.

"You have returned," he said, arching his eyebrow as he regarded me. He walked towards me and offered his hand for me to shake. I stared at it for a moment, and then I accepted it, afraid of what it would mean for me if I didn't. His grip on my hand was firm. I felt the bones in my fingers click under pressure.

Collette's words rung in my ears. *You're part of our world now. And we'll take care of you.*

Leonard released my hand. "I expect my Collette has filled you in on everything you need to know. Is that right, my dear?" He turned to face her, his mouth crooking into a crocodile smile.

"Yes, Sire," she murmured, her eyes not meeting his.

"Excellent. Then there is no need to waste precious time on the conversation. I think it's time we show Stefan just how good this life can be."

He turned back to me, that same sinister smile fixed in place. I felt my skin start to burn beneath his gaze. Slowly, he looked me up and down, clicking his tongue as he picked me apart with his stare. "Collette," he barked out her name, snapping his fingers in her direction without ever taking his eyes off me, "I want to show our recruit just how big our family is."

I looked past Leonard to Collette, my mouth falling open.

"Yes, Sire," she said, her head bowed.

She stepped quickly to the shadowed corner of the room. As she paced towards the brickwork, the air bent and twisted before her, and Collette vanished into it, melting into the nothingness.

Leonard wasted no time in taking her seat beside the fire. "By the end of tonight," he said to me, laying his arms on the armrests and leaning back, "the urge will become too much to bear." He tapped a long finger to his lips. "I predict that by sundown, you will already be your new self."

I couldn't stop myself from replying, "I don't want this. I don't want any of this." I swallowed. "I don't want to hurt anyone."

He gave way to a light laugh. "Trust me; when you get a taste, you won't be worrying about whether it hurts them or not." He stared at me for a long moment, smirking. "I see something in you, Stefan," he murmured. "What is that? A glint of intrigue perhaps?"

I shook my head, groping for words.

"You want to have power," he said, his voice making my skin crawl. "You want eternal life, strength, beauty…"

I flinched.

"You're hungry, aren't you, Stefan?" he asked.

I was. It was as though something inside of me was screaming, alive with urgency.

"It's started," Leonard told me, answering my unspoken thoughts. "Just give into it, and then you'll be free. You'll be like us."

Like them.

I caught sight of movement in the corner of the room and Collette emerged from the shadows. She was wearing black leather trousers now and a matching top, like a second skin around her pale flesh.

Leonard eyed her with approval. "Better," he said. "Now move, New Blood," he ordered me. "We have somewhere to be." He stood up and gripped my arm.

"Where are you taking me?" I asked, my eyes landing on Collette.

She gave me an almost imperceptible nod.

It was strange, but her presence still calmed me somehow. It was an odd feeling to have, considering everything that I knew. Considering everything that she'd done to me.

But it was Leonard who whispered into my ear, "You'll see soon enough."

It was almost impossible to see more than three feet in front of me. The bar was dark and full of bodies knocking into me and blocking my path. I could feel Collette behind me as I followed Leonard through the crowd. People started to the part when they noticed Leonard approach, allowing him space to walk freely ahead. I noticed some bow their heads at the sight of him.

This place was nothing like the campus bar or the Briarwood nightclubs where I'd met Will. The energy here was different, congested, dark, and the people were cold, their gazes ravenous. I caught the glowing crimson gaze of an older female and noticed the two-pointed teeth that overlapped her bottom lip. I kept my eyes trained on the floor after that, numbly trailing Leonard towards the back of the smoky establishment.

"Don't be so afraid," Collette whispered into my ear as we forged our path through the crowd. "They can sense fear. They feed off it."

If her comment was meant to help, it failed. Big time.

Ahead of us, a section of the bar was cordoned off by a red rope. A woman in a metallic-looking dress and a man in a black suit guarded the VIP area. The woman unhooked the rope at the sight of Leonard and gestured for us to pass through. She clipped the rope back onto the pole once all three of us were inside the secluded area. Leonard took a seat at one of the private booths. He reclined back on the leather bench and put his boots up on the glass table. Collette perched uncomfortably beside him and signalled with her eyes for me to do the same.

I slid into a seat beside her and clenched my teeth.

A few moments later, a barman approached our table, tray in hand. He was a weedy looking guy, pale and sweaty. I could tell by the eager glint in his sunken eyes that he was excited to be serving us, and by the way, his hands trembled as he set down three iced whiskeys on our table.

Once he finished, he stood tall and waited, hovering at our booth with a hopeful expression.

Leonard dropped his feet down from the table. "Come here," Leonard commanded, curling his finger inward. The barman stepped closed to him, then knelt before him and closed his eyes.

Collette turned her gaze away, staring at her whiskey glass, but I couldn't tear my eyes from the scene playing out before me. Leonard leaned forward and placed a kiss on the barman's mouth. It wasn't a passionate kiss, not like the kisses I'd shared with Will. Leonard's cool eyes were open as he held his lips to the barman's mouth. Then he pulled back, and with him came tendrils of black smoke, pulled from the barman's mouth. The barman let out a choked sound, as though he were gasping for air. I almost cried out as I watched Leonard draw the breath from the barman's body. And then, suddenly, everything stopped.

"Leave," Leonard said simply, his voice cold.

The barman, stunned, staggered to his feet and stumbled away from our table.

I recoiled in my seat.

Leonard took a slow swig of whiskey. "Once humans get a taste," he murmured, "they can't get enough. Filthy." He trailed his thumb over the rim of the whiskey glass, then drained the rest of the drink.

I stared at him, dumbstruck.

He ran his tongue over his teeth as he looked at Collette and me. "Drink," he said in a deep voice.

I looked down into my glass. Ice cubes danced in the amber liquid. Was it even whiskey? Now I was beginning to wonder.

"You don't have to drink it," Collette whispered into my ear. "Not if you don't want to."

Leonard slammed his hand on the table and bellowed, "Who are *you* to undermine *me*? I said *drink*."

I froze, and Collette let out a gasp. Her raven hair fell forward onto her face as she bowed closer to the table, cowering from him. A few bystanders turned to look at us with sneers on their faces, clearly entertained by Leonard's anger, clearly ravening for more.

Leonard clasped his hand around Collette's face, forcing her gaze up to him. "You," his hissed, "are *my* child. I am your Sire. You may have sired *this*," he crooked a finger in my direction. "But you are not a master. You understand me?

"Yes," she rasped. "Yes, Sire."

He bared his teeth. "Never disrespect me again."

I could see his grasp tightening around her face, and she was shaking, terrified.

"I'll drink it," I blurted out, steering Leonard's focus back to me. "It's fine." I knocked back the whiskey and tried not to grimace as the alcohol stung the back of my throat.

Leonard cricked his neck and relaxed into a smile.

Something was unnerving about the way the drink coated the burning hunger within me. Almost as though it had numbed it, or dulled it, at least.

Another round of drinks made it to us we sat in silence as the night unfolded. Leonard's stare moved sinuously over the crowd, taking everything in. As for Collette, she wouldn't look my way; her gaze stayed latched to the table.

After the third drink, it wasn't only my hunger that had dulled— so did my desire to leave. All thoughts of Phoebe, May, and Michael, the Guardians gradually melted away. I remembered them, in a hazy, distant way, but I no longer felt the urgency to get back to them. *And why should I?* I thought now, my stomach tightening. *Phoebe lied to me. She told me that death was the only option.* She'd been willing to let me die. Well, maybe I *did* have another option. At least here, tonight, there was another option.

I swallowed hard as I looked out into the seedy crowd, all moving in time to a pulse of the music. Like it or not, I was here. I was in this, and worse, I realised…it was in me.

"Look what the hounds dragged in," Leonard's voice jolted me from my reverie. I followed his gaze to the woman heading in our direction through the smoky air.

Amerie. My heart started beating faster.

Her long flaxen hair swayed as she walked our way. She moved like water through the crowd, her slip dress clinging to the curves of her body. And the moment she stepped into the soft glow of the VIP lights, I noticed something chilling.

Amerie's lips were deep red. It could have almost passed as lipstick if it wasn't for the dribble leaving a red track on her chin.

It was blood.

My hands started to shake around my whiskey glass, my mind blurry from the intoxicating drink.

Blood. Amerie was a vampire. That's what Collette had told me, and now I could see it, right before my eyes.

"Leo," Amerie purred as she slipped into the seat between Leonard and Collette, the hem of her dress riding up to her thigh. "What a surprise to see you tonight."

Leonard simply arched an eyebrow.

Amerie trailed her fingers along his jawline, then slid her hand down his shirt and over the zipper on his jeans. "I've haven't seen you here in a long time," Amerie simpered. "I thought this wasn't your scene. I do hope my children have made you feel very welcome. *You*, at least." Her hand moved lithely over his jacket.

Leonard pushed her hand away. The relaxed expression no longer painted on his face. Instead, he snarled as he locked eyes with her.

"I can bring my children here if I so choose," Leonard said, and I flinched when I realised that he was referring to Collette and me. His children?

Amerie threw back her head and laughed. "*Your* children? This one is yours," she said, pointing a long fingernail towards Collette. "But this one," her finger moved to me, "is hers."

A wave of nausea washed over me. Amerie's focus was on me now. Everyone's was. Collette had sired me— *she'd* been the one to turn me into an Incubus. So that made me, what? Collette's property?

"He's mine," Leonard seethed through gritted teeth. "She may have sired him, but he belongs to me now. He's under my control."

I held my breath, afraid of what would happen next.

Amerie sat up straighter, gone was the playfulness of her demeanour. "Watch your tone," she spat. "This is a place for vampires, not your rogue soul suckers. Haven't we spoke about staying out of each other's way? We wouldn't want any more *little* accidents now, would we?" Her eyes wandered to me, and I looked away.

Vampires, I realised. The people in the bar were all vampires. Suddenly I felt as though the walls were closing in on me. Hundreds of sets of scarlet eyes, noticing me, watching me, waiting for me to step closer to them.

"Now, Amerie," Leonard drawled, at ease again. "There's no need to be hostile. You always were snappy after a feed." He leaned in closer to her and licked a smear of blood from the corner of her mouth.

Disgust rolled like a wave in my stomach.

I turned to Collette, and she stared helplessly back at me.

"Leonard," another voice snapped all four of our attention across the VIP area. "Drop that. You don't know where it's been."

A younger guy was heading towards us. The VIP security unhooked the rope to grant him access. He was handsome, dark hair and a little stubble along his jaw. He couldn't have been much older than me, and even in the dim lighting, I could see the glow of his golden eyes.

Incubus eyes, I recognised.

Leonard and Amerie turned to him, silently.

"I've been looking for you, Leo," he said, stalking towards our booth.

For the first time even, Leonard looked uncomfortable. Powerless, almost. "Sam," he greeted the newcomer. "I thought you were out of town."

Sam's gaze flickered to me for a moment. "Well, I'm back. We need to talk."

Collette cowered in her seat, her hands balled into fists as she rocked back and forth.

Who was this guy?

Leonard cleared his throat. "Collette, my love, take Stefan back to the warehouse."

Her voice trembled. "But, Sire, I—"

"*Now*," Leonard barked. His eyes never left Sam, his mouth twisted into a sinister smile.

I felt woozy as Collette pulled me to my feet and guided me towards a door at the back of the VIP area. Glancing over my shoulder, I noticed the same opaque smoke I'd seen leave the barman's mouth dance in Leonard's palm as he eyeballed Sam.

"What's going on?" I murmured to Collette as we made for the exit.

"It doesn't matter," she said. "We need to leave."

Suddenly there was a commotion across the bar. Lights danced on the walls and ceiling, and screams began to erupt.

"Guardians!" someone hollered.

Collette's grip tightened as she shoved me to the door.

Leonard, Amerie and Sam jumped to their feet, their eyes trained on the blinding lights in the bar area. Leonard's threw his arms wide and black smoke poured from his body, darkening the whole area.

Collette dragged me to the back exit. Stunned, I tried to turn to see the three we'd left behind, but once she ushered me through the door, the floor fell from under my feet, and I landed on my hands and knees back in the warehouse.

CHAPTER TWENTY

"What the hell happened back there?" I shouted at Collette. My heart was beating fast, pumping double time.

"I don't know," Collette said, running her fingers quickly through her hair as we stood alone in the dull room in the warehouse. "It happens. There are Guardians everywhere…"

Guardians. My thoughts jumped back to Phoebe and her family, and my stomach knotted at the thought that it could have been them in the bar. I don't know who I was more afraid for, Phoebe in a bar full of vampires, or myself in a room full of Guardians. After all, I was just another Demon now, wasn't I? To them, at least.

"We have to be careful when we feed," Collette said, wringing out her hands. "Maybe they were following Amerie. The Guardians would need no excuse to slaughter us all though."

I shook my head in disbelief. "Can you blame them? You're talking about *feeding*," I echoed her wording with revulsion. "You're talking about killing, taking human lives, like it's okay. Like it's normal."

"We don't kill," Collette snapped back. "Not all of us. After the first transition, we don't need to kill to survive. It's a choice. It's a compulsion, and you can choose to ignore it."

I didn't believe for a second that Amerie hadn't killed someone tonight. I'd seen the murderous look inside her blood-red eyes.

"I can't do this," I murmured. "I can't *be* this."

"It's too late," she said. "It's either become one or—"

"I know," I cut her off. "Or die."

Silence hung between us, and the crackle of the dying embers of the fire sounded deafening in my ears. I rubbed my temples. My head was throbbing.

"What was in those drinks?" I asked, my voice scratchy. "It wasn't just whiskey, was it?"

Collette cast her gaze the floor. "It's an enactment, like a drug. It's supposed to sedate you. I don't know," she sighed, "Leonard wants to lure you into this world, but he wants it on his terms."

I grimaced. Even if I had felt sedated in the bar, that certainly wasn't the case now.

"You're sick and twisted," I muttered. "All of you."

"You think I wanted this?" Collette said, at last, drawing my gaze back to her. "You think I chose this?"

I gritted my teeth and said nothing.

"I didn't," she said emphatically. "I was as much a mistake as you were. Leonard didn't intend to sire me, but he did. It happened. I was just a soul filth, like the barman we saw tonight. I was a dumb girl who thrived off the *rush* of an Incubus. Leonard breathed into me because I begged him to."

I turned away from her in disgust.

"But Leonard took it too far one night," she went on. "He almost killed me—he *could* have killed me if he'd wanted to. But he stopped himself. He brought me back from the brink. So then, just like you, I was left worse off than death."

A deranged laugh slipped past my lips, "I'm not like you," I said, my voice hollow. "I'm nothing like you. Because I won't choose to kill to satisfy my survival."

"That's what I thought, too," she murmured. "That's what I kept telling myself—"

I raised my palm to stop her. "This may have happened to me," I accepted, "but I'm not going to make the choices you've made. If I can't live without killing someone, then I won't live at all." I moved to the door.

"You can't keep running away from this," Collette called after me. "You may think you're stronger than me, better than me. But remember, I was where you are, not so long ago. I know how hard it is to ignore the urge. It only gets worse."

I cringed, trying to block out the gripping hunger inside of me.

"I was strong," she said.

I didn't turn back as I replied, "But I'm stronger."

Chapter Twenty-One

I hovered on the staircase with my hand folded over the oak rail. Dad stepped into the house and shrugged out of his coat. He hung it on the rack and let out a slow breath. I don't think he realised that I was watching him.

"Where have you been?" my voice sprung from the shadows on the lamp-lit staircase.

Dad turned and looked up at me from the hallway. "I was following a lead," he said. "There's a bar in Colmark, just off the highway. A few of the ministry were tracking vampires…"

A Guardian ambush on an underground bar? It wasn't like my dad to get involved in that kind of thing.

"Brave," I said quietly. I was unable to hide the note of irony in my tone. Stupid, more like. What was he thinking?

And then it made sense. *Of course*. I swallowed. Dad was looking for the liar. They all were. Well, a vamp bar off Route 6 sure as hell wasn't it.

Footsteps thudded on the upper floor and Mum appeared at the top of the staircase.

"Michael," she breathed as she rushed down the stairs, sidling past me.

"May." He met her in the hallway and wrapped his arms around her, his tall frame enveloping her. "Don't worry. I'm fine. Everything's fine."

"There were too many," she said, her voice muffled as she spoke into his shoulder. "I saw it in a vision, but I was too late to warn you. I was too late."

He stroked her silver hair, soothing her. My shoulders tensed.

"Any casualties?" I asked. The words sounded far away, lost somewhere in time.

Dad met my eyes over Mum's shoulder, his arms still locked around her. "Yes," he said, sombre. "There are always some."

A Guardian died tonight. Maybe more than one. I could feel the admission pulsing on his energy.

Mum slipped free of him. She turned to me now. They both did. "Please, Phoebe," she whispered. "Please. Let's end this."

How many more people had to die before I gave the game up? How many lives lost already?

What was I fighting for? Sam? Stef?

Myself?

And then the words just escaped, as if they'd found their way to the surface, defying whatever messed up logic had kept them hidden for so many years.

"There's a warehouse," I said in a trembling breath. "On the border of Briarwood and West Haven. It's hidden in marshland." There. The words were out, and they were cold and black, and broken.

I watched my mother nearly crumple to the floor in relief, and my father exhales for what seemed like the first time in years.

It was over.

I didn't hang around after that. I couldn't. It was all I could do to make it to my bedroom and collapse onto the floor, silent tears spilling down my cheeks and a knot of grief twisting inside of me. Well, that was that. They knew where the illusive hideout was now. They'd slay Stef if it were not already too late. They were just doing what we do; killing demons. They were stopping this from happening to any more innocent people.

Now they knew, would they kill them all. Leonard, Sam, Stef. Part of me hoped they'll have time to escape. My fleeting thought goes against everything I know.

All of a sudden, I couldn't breathe. My chest tightened, squeezing the air from my lungs. I staggered to my feet and threw open the window onto the cold night. My eyes held the full moon as it blurred my tears. I let out a cry—a hopeless, shattered cry.

I wanted to scream. To all of *them*. I was sorry. My parents, Stef, Sam, and all the lost lives because I'd refused to betray Sam.

145

But it was all over now.

Some way in the distance, I hear a scream, and another, and another moving like a ripple, a brewing tsunami on the horizon. And they were screaming only for my ears.

I shivered in the icy air. Something moved over my skin, spreading goose pimples along my arms.

The screams grew louder, more piercing.

I pressed my hands over my ears, trying to block out the bone-shuddering wails. But no amount of dulling could block their cries. I yanked the window shut and sank to the floor, breathless.

The Banshees were coming. It was warning of death.

A massacre was on its way.

Lilith's third child, born from her cries of pain. The mysterious third demon race had arrived at last. Guardians had been waiting for this day to come.

Chapter Twenty-Two

I ran from the warehouse, following the route I'd taken with Phoebe just a day earlier. Although now, it felt like a lifetime had passed since yesterday. Perhaps, in some ways, it had.

The moon hung full in the sky and the clear ebony night made the stars stand out brighter than I'd ever seen before. My phone wasn't in my pocket like it usually was, I guess it was lost somewhere inside the office at school, where I'd last spoken to Phoebe. I kept pacing along the tree-bound road, my thoughts jumbled, and my body is churning with changes.

At last, I reached a part of town I recognised, and I let my instinct guide me towards Will's house. I had to see him. I had to see someone who wasn't a Demon, or a Guardian, or anything other than a familiar face.

As I waded through the remnants of snow on the pavement, I realised that the cold wasn't affecting me as it had done before. My bare arms didn't bother me, and there was no numbness in my face as I walked through the biting wind. It made sense. I was changing.

All I knew for sure was that in a couple of days I'd be dead. I guess nothing else mattered after that.

I rounded a corner on the suburban street, and Will's house came into view. The first-floor window where Will's bedroom was, gave off a soft glow, a beacon in the otherwise dark night.

I emptied my mind as I crept onto the front lawn, concealed from the road by hedges and rose bushes. I searched blindly for something to throw at the window and stopped when my fingers grazed over a small stone. I weighed it in my hand and then, holding my breath, I threw it.

The stone tapped on the windowpane. I starred up, waiting for a sign that it had caught Will's attention. Seconds passed in agonising concession before a silhouette moved behind the curtains. One of the curtains peeled back, and Will's face appeared. His expression relaxed when his eyes landed on me. He signalled for me to go to the front door, just like he'd done dozens of times before.

By the time I reached the porch, the front door was already opening, and Will was waiting in the dark corridor. His bare chest caught me by surprise. Even in the darkness, I could see the defined lines that were mapped out on his skin like a jigsaw puzzle—one that I wanted to touch. I shook the thought aside and looked up as he mouthed for me to follow him.

It wasn't that his parents didn't approve of me—at least, I didn't think they did—it was more they didn't approve of these late-night visits. But that had never stopped us. And right now, I didn't feel an ounce of guilt as I made my way up the stairs towards his room. I needed him.

Will closed the bedroom door behind us and turned to me. "I've been trying to call you all day," he murmured. "Where have you been hiding?"

I clenched my teeth, suppressing a grimace.

"I've been at Phoebe's," I said. "I should have called, but we've been so busy with school work..." My lie couldn't come out fast enough.

Will pulled a face, one side of his mouth turning down and the opposite eyebrow lifted up. "I spoke to Phoebe," he said in a discerning voice. "She told me she hadn't seen you. Don't lie to me, Stef. If something has happed... if you've met someone else—"

"No," I said, shaking my head. "No, it's nothing like that." I broke eye contact and walked over to his bed, exhaustion gripping a tight hold on my legs. Honestly, I didn't know what to say to him, but I could feel his gaze begging for answers, demanding them. Part of me wanted to tell him the truth, blurt out everything about Collette, and Leonard, and what was happening to me. But he'd think I was crazy. I mean, I hardly believed it myself, and I was the one *living* it.

"If you're seeing someone else, Stef," he said again. "I'd rather just know. I'm a big boy; I can handle it."

"No," I told him again. "I swear to you, I'm not." I sat down on his bed and raked my hands through my hair. "It's just been a weird day. I've got a lot on my mind."

He stepped closer to me. "You can talk to me," he said. "That's why you're here, right?" He reached out and trailed a finger down my cheek. "Unless you're here for something else." His expression turned playful, lust shining in his eyes. The bed shifted as he sat down next to me. He placed a hand on my stomach and rubbed his thumb in circles over my abdomen.

I found myself shying away from him.

"Will," I said, placing my hand on his. Sudden desire to taste him overtook me. I gazed into his knowing eyes, and we moved to each other.

I opened my mouth to speak, but he kissed me, a slow, passionate kiss. I felt myself melt into him, overcome by desire for him. I rolled over as my jeans were peeled off. They landed on the floor, and Will's strong hand turned me to face him. The bed jumped as he dropped down close to my lips. His hands braced on either side of me. I gave in to the pull of lust and lifted my mouth to his. His tongue moved with mine, and I felt the stiff lump of something press against my bare leg. Need to be burned through me.

I wrapped my legs around his waist and heaved my body up until he was under me. My hands ran over his chest and around his neck. Our kisses intensified, mirrored by the growing hunger.

A distant voice in my subconscious recoiled away from this feeling. Something about this passion, this insatiable hunger, felt dark, wrong. But I couldn't stop, kissing hard, gripping tighter. A wave of pressure was building within me, one that I had no control over. I was being pulled by the tidal wave, drowning in its clutches. I grabbed onto Will's strong arms, holding him in place as I lusted for more. My tongue played with his; hands exploring every inch of his body.

I lost grip on time and reality. Then, Collette's face flashed through my mind. My eyes shot open, only to see the horror inches from my face.

Consumed by lust, I hadn't noticed how still Will had become. His face was rigid; eyes were frozen open, lips saint blue. A spasm of pain erupted through my spine, and I fell to the floor. The lights above me blinked as I gasped for breath and, for a split second, darkness swallowed the room.

All I felt was a pain; hot and searing. My limbs felt as though they were twisted, and the hollowness inside of me was full, ready to burst. I was full, for the first time in days, the hunger vacant, replaced with an entirely new sensation.

I wanted to scream.

The room came to life again, bright now, blindingly bright. From where I lay, I saw the bedroom door open, and two figures hovering beneath the doorframe with ashen faces. Was it two? My vision was blurry; everything was out of focus.

I scrambled back, away from the Will's lifeless body.

"It is complete."

The voice was muffled, but it was close to me, almost inside of me. It was rich, deep... *Leonard*. My eyes wouldn't focus.

Will. Will. Will.

I felt his soul swirl around me, filling that space; quenching the hunger.

My vision began to restore, the pain faltering into nothingness. Leonard came into focus, a smile crooked onto his handsome face. I looked at the figure behind him and now saw Collette standing amongst the dancing shadow. It was all so clear. It was all so *real*.

Collette wasn't looking at me. She was looking at the body splayed on the bed. I followed her gaze until my eyes rested on Will's face. Now, in the clarity, I could see the whispers of white smoke that floated from his slack mouth, stark against his greying skin.

I stood, using the wall to pull myself up. I stepped closer to the bed. I knew what waited for me, what I'd done. I could smell it, taste the death on my tongue.

I'd killed him.

Grief bubbled within me, but the swirling soul overpowered that emotion, muddling everything. I wanted to cry, to scream, to beg for forgiveness and mercy, but I could only stare.

I pressed my hand to Will's strong face, feeling the chill of death.

Me, the killer.

Will, my prey.

"What have I done?" I directed my words like sharp knifes towards Leonard. I didn't take my eyes off Will as I spoke. "That drink you gave me... You drugged me—"

Leonard rumbled with laughter. "The drink was merely a tonic. A gift to help you on your way. As for this," he gestured towards Will, "I had no hand in this. This is *all* you, New Blood. And might I say, what an attractive choice you made." He leered at Will's motionless body, arching an eyebrow in approval.

"Don't you dare!" I turned to him, my voice raising. The light bulb flickered again, and the shadows danced faster. "Don't you dare even look at him!"

Collette recoiled from me, and Leonard continued to laugh. Deep, resounding laughter.

There was a knock on the bedroom door. "Will?" My blood chilled at the sound of Will's mum's gentle voice on the other side of the door. "What is going on in there?"

Leonard stared at the close door and ran his tongue across his teeth.

"Don't," I warned, pre-empting his thoughts.

His smirked. "Watching you feed has made me hungry. I'm in the mood for a snack."

"Leonard..." Collette choked. "Please."

The door creaked open, and Will's mum appeared. Her eyes landed on me first. Her mouth fell open, but she faltered when she saw Leonard and Collette. Her face paled as her gaze landed on Will.

Then, Leonard attacked.

The scream ripped through my throat. I lunged forward, moving with speed. In a second, I was standing before Will's mum, using all my strength to push Leonard back. To my surprise, he flew across the room, colliding into the window and exploding it into thousands of glinting fragments of glass.

Collette drew in a breath as Leonard dissipated before falling from the shattered window. He materialized back in the centre of the room, unharmed.

Will's mum was screaming at me, and I barely had a chance to register the sight of Will's dad dragging her from the bedroom before my vision flashed white. I stumbled to the floor, looking up just in time to see the boot come for my face. My head snapped back, and my stomach turned, but the pain was nothing compared to what I'd already faced. I sprung to my feet and grabbed the back of Leonard's jacket. He was halfway out the door, going after Will's parents, but I pulled him back. My arms burned with new found strength and I threw Leonard to the floor.

"You'll leave them." I hissed. It surprised me when he stopped fighting, his golden eyes glowing up at me.

"If I can't have *them*," he murmured darkly, "then I'll just take yours." That familiar smirked curved onto his lips.

Leonard took a shuddering breath, and the swirling soul that had embedded itself within me began to rush from my body. I watched, eyes wide, as the white smoke seeped from my mouth into Leonards. At that moment,

I lost control of my body and gave in to the darkness that crept into the corners of my eyes.

CHAPTER TWENTY-THREE

I knelt on my bedroom floor at my parent's house; a crumpled road map spread out across the rug.

Jeanie's ethereal form was pacing around the room; her translucent hands pressed delicately to her ears.

"What's happening?" she asked, her voice wavering. "Why are they screaming?" Her pretty face creased in pain. "Why won't they stop?"

I swallowed. For the past few minutes, I'd been trying in vain to block out the sound of her voice. I needed to focus. But maintaining concertation was hard when there was a neurotic spirit trampling through me every few seconds.

"It's the banshees; I explained, distractedly. "The banshees are coming."

"What does that mean, *the banshees are coming?*" she echoed my words back to me. She'd stopped pacing, and her hands were on her hips.

I grimaced. "It means death is on the way. Big time."

Jeanie let out a small whimper, following by a long, drawn-out wail of distress. "It's happening," she bemoaned. "It's starting. The demons are waging war. It started with me, and now *him*. Stefan."

I gritted my teeth. For a rookie ghost, Jeanie was intuitive. It was what *I* was afraid of too. So, Stefan had chosen death? Maybe that was it. Honestly, I didn't think I could stomach the thought of the alternative right now.

Jeanie gave way to another breathy cry. "The bloodshed... The *bloodshed*! I can't stand it!"

I tuned out the sound of her haunted wails and stared down at the open map.

Okay. Breathe.

I let all my fear and nervousness slip from my mind as I hovered my palms above the Briarwood road atlas.

My chest began to feel warm, a comforting pulse of heat that cossetted my heart. The sensation moved along my arms, finally reaching my fingers, and I murmured the words, "Find Stefan."

A bolt of light shot from my hands and sparked on the page.

I'd found him.

I pinned my fingertip to the location as the pearl of light fizzled away.

Marlon Terrace. I knew that street name. I'd given Stefan a ride there a couple of times this year.

Will, I realised at once.

So, Stef was at Will's house.

Stef, the transitioning, lust-filled almost-Incubus, was at his boyfriend Will's house.

Oh. God.

My hands gripped the steering wheel, and I pressed my foot down on the gas pedal. I sped down the suburban road, and beneath my tight grasp, the wheel juddered and trembled. In the black night, streetlamp's bulbs flashed intermittently as I passed each one by, blinking in and out in time with my pounding heartbeat.

I swerved onto Marlon Terrace and pulled up alongside the curb, where hedges and rose bushes flanked a neat lawn.

Will's house.

I cut the engine and stared out at the darkened house. The lights were all out, and the curtains were drawn. Of course, what else had I expected? It was past midnight.

But Stef was in there, somewhere. At least, this is where my scrying had led me. Whether he was *still* in there, remained to be seen.

I opened the Chevy's door with a creak and winced as I stepped out into the icy night.

In a stupor, I walked along the pathway leading to the front door. My pulse quickened when I noticed that the door was already open, swaying gently in the breeze and tapping against the latch.

Biting my lip, I nudged the door a little wider and stepped through the threshold.

"Hello?" I murmured into the dark house. "Is anyone here?"

There was no response, apart from the brassy thrum of a grandfather clock somewhere inside the hallway.

This wasn't good. This wasn't good at all.

"Hello?" I called a little louder.

My voice sounded deafening in the stillness of the house. There was no sound of movement or life anywhere.

In my experience, that was always a bad sign.

I fumbled my way through the lower hallway, trailing my fingers over the wall as I searched blindly for a light switch. At last, I felt the raised switch and flipped it. But the bulbs overhead just clicked, unresponsive.

So, either the power was out, or an overload of demonic energy had blown a fuse.

I was willing to bet on the latter.

Time for Plan B.

I extended my hand and drew in a deep, steadying breath. Slowly, a ball of reflective light began to take shape in my palm, twirling into an orb. The revolving sphere gave off just enough light for me to manoeuvre a path up the staircase.

I began up the steps. There was something at the top, a silhouette in the darkness, but low to the ground. I lingered on the staircase and raised the orb a little higher to illuminate the shape.

It was a person. A woman. She was lying in the upper hallway, her arm draped down onto the staircase, fingers skimming the banister.

I ran up the last few steps and crouched beside her, checking for a pulse on her wrist.

Nothing.

My stomach lurched. She was dead.

My gaze shot to the upper hallway and my eyes landed on another motionless body—a man, this time—lying in the corridor.

Two dead.

With my heart hammering in my throat, I nudged open the nearest door and lifted my hand to illuminate the room. At once, I saw Will, reclined shirtless on his bed, his eyes wide open and his lips parted.

I heaved.

They were all dead. So, Stefan had been here. And, evidentially, he had chosen a side.

I squashed my hand into a fist, snuffing out the light.

I couldn't look anymore.

CHAPTER TWENTY-FOUR

The scream ripped through my throat. I lunged forward, moving with speed. In a second, I was standing before Will's mum, using all my strength to push Leonard back. To my surprise, he flew across the room, colliding into the window and exploding it into thousands of glinting fragments of glass.

Collette drew in a breath as Leonard dissipated before falling from the shattered window. He materialized back in the centre of the room, unharmed.

Will's mum was screaming at me, and I barely had a chance to register the sight of Will's dad dragging her from the bedroom before my vision flashed white. I stumbled to the floor, looking up just in time to see the boot come for my face. My head snapped back, and my stomach turned, but the pain was nothing compared to what I'd already faced. I sprung to my feet and grabbed the back of Leonard's jacket. He was halfway out the door, going after Will's parents, but I pulled him back.

My arms burned with new found strength and I threw Leonard to the floor.

"You'll leave them." I hissed. It surprised me when he stopped fighting, his golden eyes glowing up at me.

"If I can't have *them*," he murmured darkly, "then I'll just take yours." That familiar smirked curved onto his lips.

Leonard took a shuddering breath, and the swirling soul that had embedded itself within me began to rush from my body. I watched, eyes wide, as the white smoke flowed from my mouth into Leonard's. At that moment, I lost control of my body and gave in to the darkness that crept into the corners of my eyes.

When I regained consciousness, I was on a table. I didn't need to open my eyes to feel the restraints holding my wrists and ankles down. An intense throbbing coated my entire skull, and my body felt alien as I lay still, trying to make sense of where I was. Of *who* I was.

I tried to move, yanking at my arms and legs. But I was trapped. Caught in Leonards web.

"Where am I?" I mumbled. My voice sounded hoarse. "What happened?" My eyes stung as I tried to open them. It was as though the lashes had soldered together.

"Steady…" Collette's voice came from somewhere above me. Hazy, I peered up at her from where I lay.

"Did he kill them?" I struggled to free myself from the restraints on my wrists.

"Take it easy," Collette murmured, touching my face with her delicate hand. "I need you to listen to me. Any minute now Leonard is going to come back here, and you are going to have to play along with everything he says. You understand?"

I shook my head, panic growing as I struggled against the binds. "What happened? I don't...I don't remember."

"It will all come back to you," she said. "For now, stop fighting and just listen. If you want to get out of here, you need to play along."

I did as she asked, laying still on the table. Her golden eyes soothed me, and a familiar instinct guided me to trust her, to obey her. It was stronger now, though. The instinct, I mean. It was as though I was no longer just influenced by her. Moreover, I was wired to submit to her.

I gritted my teeth. *No... No, I can fight this...*

"Remember," she whispered. "Play along."

I held her gaze as a door banged open somewhere inside the room.

Leonard strolled into my line of vision, his expression aloof.

I looked helplessly up at him from where I lay.

"Oh, good," he uttered darkly. "You're awake. I was hoping we could have a little chat, you and me." He took my face in his hand and squeezed. "How does that sound, New Blood?"

Collette's words echoed in my foggy mind, *Play along.*

I managed to nod my head, and Leonard released me from his vice-like grip.

"I don't like being disobeyed," Leonard said, his face close to mine. "And that stunt you pulled at your dearly departed house has caused me some concern."

"What...?" I blinked, trying to recall a dream or a memory... *Will*, I remembered. A vision of Will's bedroom flashed through my mind, then his lifeless body beneath me... The fight with Leonard. Will's parents.

My chest tightened, and tears started to burn in my eyes. *No.* No, this couldn't be real.

Leonard sneered at me. "Thanks to you, the Guardians are on our tail."

"You were going to hurt them," I couldn't hide the seething in my voice. "Will's parents...Have you...? Did you hurt them?"

Leonard laughed under his breath. "But, you see, I had to. I did it for you."

My heart gave a heavy thud. "You're a monster," I choked. "They were good people, innocent people."

He ran his tongue over his teeth. "Everyone's innocent once. Anyway, your prey's parents would have identified you at the murder scene; we had to get them out of the picture before they started running their mouths. Lucky for you, I was on hand to clean up your mess."

A tear rolled onto my cheek.

"So," Leonard said, pushing his hand down upon my chest until my spine ached on the metal table, "are you going to behave? Or am I going to have to teach you a lesson in who's running this town?"

I gasped for air.

"No more little outbursts?" he said, his nails digging into my shirt. "No more disobeying your master?"

I coughed out a noise, between a yes and a cry for help.

"Good." Leonard released his hold on me. "Collette," he signalled across the room. "Keep New Blood under control until I get back."

Collette took a cautious step forward. "Where are you going?"

"I have business to arrange. And Sam and I need to discuss this little problem you've created. It seems like my other sister has arrived in town with her children and I don't like that." His eyes lingered on me for a moment longer.

Collette shivered. "What if the Guardians come here?" she asked. "What should I do?"

"They won't come here," Leonard muttered. "We have Demon's watching our boundaries. No one's getting in here tonight. Well, no one's getting in *alive*, anyway."

On his final word, there was a rush of air, and he vanished in a bend of darkness.

As soon as Leonard was gone, I gave way to a ragged breath. Collette stepped towards me. Without a word, she removed the binds from my legs and arms and helped me to my feet. I staggered down from the table, and Collette gripped my arm to steady me.

"You need to go," she whispered. "You need to get out of here before Leonard comes back."

My eyes adjusted to the hollow room of the warehouse. "How? You heard Leonard; his Demons are watching the place. No one can get past them." I tried again to pull out of the straps.

"They're watching the entrances," Collette said. "But there's a way out, through the portal."

"Portal?" My eyes shot to the shadowed corner that Leonard had disappeared into.

"There are portals everywhere," she said. "You just have to learn how to sense them. You have to get to the Guardians."

I choked out a breath. "Are you insane? The Guardians will kill me. I did it; I made the kill. I'm an Incubus now." The word stuck in my throat. Saying it out loud was like a bolt through my chest. I was an Incubus, and I'd killed Will.

Collette shook her head. "You'll be safe with her, the girl that came to you before. I overheard Leonard talking, and he's scared of her, I think. She has some sort of power over him, some way of stopping him. We have to tell her that Leonard is forming an army, but you're not part of it."

Her words seemed to jumble in my head. "What do you mean? I...I don't understand."

"She'll know what to do," Collette said, snapping the ties from around my arms and legs. "The Guardian girl."

"Phoebe?" I stammered. "You mean Phoebe?"

I sat up, stretching the ache in my body.

Collette grabbed hold of my arm and pulled me towards the corner of the room where the shadows clustered. I let her lead me as her words bounced around in my already tangled mind. I knew what I'd done, and I knew what it meant. I gave in to the hunger, the desire, and I killed Will. There was no turning back now.

Phoebe would never forgive me for this.

I would never forgive myself.

The air changed, wrapping around Collette and me as we stepped into the shadows of the room. Suddenly my entire body felt weightless.

"Take us there," Collette's voice rang in my ears. "Take us to the Guardians. Envisage it."

On her command, I found myself picturing Phoebe's family home; the iron gates, the moss on the ground, the stone pathway leading to the gothic house…

I watched in awe as the shadows wound around us and the images beyond morphed. We were no longer in the barren warehouse; we transported to the place I'd manifested.

Now, we stood at the iron gates of Phoebe's family home. Heavy snow was falling around us, blanketing the ground. The icy air didn't touch me though, it curled around me, my skin hot.

Collette pushed against the gates, and they groaned open. "I can take you to the Guardians, but I won't stay. They won't allow it. You're on your own after this."

I hesitated. "Leonard will be angry," I warned her. Something pulled in my chest, a feeling of pity, or remorse. "When he finds out that you let me go, he'll be out for your blood."

She smiled sadly at me through the feathery snowflakes. "What's the worst *he* can do?" she said. "Kill me? Send me to hell?" She shrugged her thin shoulders. "I'm already there."

I took hold of her hand. "Run," I said. "You should run away. Get out of Briarwood."

"What's the point?" she murmured. "He will find me. He's my sire. But he won't find you." She met my eyes in earnest. "*I* turned you, not him. No matter how much he tries to convince himself that he's your sire, he's not. And he never will be."

"Where will you go?" I asked weakly.

She slipped free of my hand and touched her fingertips to her chest. "Back to him. What better poetry is it than to have *this* life taken by the same man who took away my last life." Her dark hair stirred in the bitter wind, snow melting into the strands.

"I'm sorry," I managed.

She bowed her head. "I'm sorry, too."

There was nothing left to say. I inhaled a deep breath, and I stepped through the gates. With Collette trailing behind me, our footsteps crunching on the snowy path, we approached the house with its towering frosted turrets. Collette stayed a few paces behind, even when we reached the porchway. I suppose she was afraid. I suppose I was, too. I tapped the brass door knocker.

I saw the blurred figure move towards us through the stained-glass panel on the door. Then, the door opened wide.

Michael stood before us, a look of shock painted on his face. His lips trembled as he searched for words. He looked at Collette and me, shaking his head.

"I hoped it wouldn't come to this," he said in a somber voice.

Collette stepped forward, her arms raised to show she was no threat. "You need to protect Stefan," she said. "Please. Leonard will be coming for him."

I caught sight of May pacing towards us through the corridor. She joined Michael in the doorway, and her eyes locked with Collette's. "I'm warning you," she said, holding a small silver pendant high. "Don't come any closer." When May looked at me, her gaze reflected the same sadness that clung to Michael. She said my name, elongating the syllables into a plea, or an apology, I wasn't sure.

"I'm not here to fight," Collette assured May. "I'm only here to ensure Stefan's safety. I know you'll protect him."

May looked at Michael, exchanging something beyond words. "We won't," she murmured at last. "We can't. It's too late. You're…"

"An Incubus," I answered for her. I could see my reflection in the silver pendant, the golden hue of my eyes was mirrored back at me.

"Stefan has chosen a side," Michael said, "and it's not our side. So, he is no longer under our protection."

Michael began to shut the door, but Collette pushed past me and held it open. "Please," she beseeched. "He doesn't deserve this. He's not one of us. He's not under Leonard's control!"

"I told you to stay back!" May shouted, and Michael raised a hand in response. Collette was knocked backwards by an invisible force, thrown down the porch steps at Michael's will.

I drew in a sharp breath, frozen in fear.

But Collette rose to her feet and met my eyes. "I'm okay," she said. "It's okay." She returned her gaze to May and Michael. "They're forming an army."

Michael lowered his gaze. "We know. You're part of it."

"But Stefan isn't. Stefan needs protecting from them," Collette implored. "He needs a chance. He's not like the rest of us. Stef was a mistake, and he can choose a better way, with your help."

"Absurd," May muttered. Her attention glued to me, but her gaze wasn't warm like it had been a week ago. "We know of another Incubus who wasn't *sired* by the great and powerful Leonard," she scoffed, "and yet he is just as culpable, and has caused just as much pain—"

"Stefan isn't Sam," Collette snapped back.

Sam? I knew that name. He'd been in the bar tonight.

"Demons are demons," May hissed. "There is no grey area."

I stood between the two warring parties, lost for words.

"Please," Collette murmured at last. "Please have mercy on him. He's just an innocent in all of this. He didn't go looking for this, not like the rest of us did."

May and Michael swapped another look, and I glanced at Collette who offered me a weak smile in response.

"Stefan may enter this house," Michael said at last. "But not you." His eyes were on Collette, unyielding. "I trust you will disappear and never return. Otherwise, you will not be treated with such leniency again."

Collette nodded. "Keep Stefan safe. I owe him this, at least." She looked at me one final time, and her whisper carried on the cold wind, "I hope you can forgive me." Then she took two steps back, turned, and walked away into the night that swallowed her whole.

Chapter Twenty-Five

I stared into the mirror that May held before me. I moved my head from side to side, wishing that the reflection wasn't mine. My eyes were the first noticeable difference. My left eye burned gold, just like Leonard's and Collette's, but my right was the same brown hue that it had always had been. I blinked, once, twice, but nothing changed.

"What does it mean?" I asked as I ran a finger beneath my golden eye.

May clicked her tongue. "I'm not sure. Maybe the transition did not complete as it should." She avoided my gaze, but I saw her grimace. She was disgusted by me. I couldn't blame her. *I* was disgusted by myself.

"Can it be reversed?" I asked feebly. "Please tell me it can!"

May said nothing. She poured me a tea and handed me the cup.

I looked away from the mirror. The sight of myself turned my stomach. "I didn't mean to do it," I whispered. "Will. I…I couldn't stop myself."

May's hand rested on my shoulder. "I know," was all she said.

"Kill me. I deserve it," my voice sounded strangled. "A life for a life."

"It's done. And you must understand that we, as Guardians, must decide on how to…On how to deal with this."

"But the one brown eye," I said, glancing back at the mirror and the familiar face trapped inside the looking-glass. "It didn't complete. Maybe I'm not a Demon. Maybe I'm just…" I let the sentence trail off. *A murderer?* Is that what I was going to say? Like that's better somehow?

"You are an Incubus," May confirmed, her tone sterile. "But you are…" her gaze lingered on my reflection, "different."

Footsteps approached, and the floorboards behind me creaked. I spun around to see Phoebe standing in the living room doorway. She hesitated when our eyes met. She just stood there, perfectly still, regarding me silently.

"Phoebe…" It was all I could say. I wanted to hug her. I wanted her to hug me. Tears blurred my vision. "Phoebe." I choked out a cry. "I'm a monster." I wanted her to hear my admission. I wanted her to help me. But she didn't move; she just watched me. "I'm sorry," I broke into sobs.

She moved so fast that I flinched, afraid of her. But she only threw her arms around me. "It's okay," she whispered, shivering. "Everything's going to be okay."

I almost laughed at the lie. Nothing was ever going to be okay again.

CHAPTER TWENTY-SIX

I stood alone in the cemetery, the snow numbing my limbs and dampening my hair. I breathed in the familiar scents of hyacinth and pine, and took in the myriad of moonlit sights that had defined my teenage years, defined my *life*. I hadn't been back here in a long time, not since I'd left him here on that final day.

Sam.

I didn't know if he'd show up. I didn't know if he'd ever show up again after that night. But I'd often wondered. Had he tried for a little while, wondering if I'd give in to temptation and show up, too? Or had he realised on the same night that I had, we were doomed.

So, why was I back here tonight? Why had I returned, a year and a half after I'd last set foot on Maura's grave? I had to see him. I had to warn him. I'd heard the banshee scream, once for Will, and once more.

And I had to warn Sam. If I wasn't already too late, that is. I guess no matter how hard I'd tried over the years; I couldn't let him go. Not fully, anyway.

I felt his presence before I saw him.

"Pheebs," he whispered my name.

I turned around, and my body went weak like I was nothing but air, and he was the fire that existed because of me.

"You're alive," I said, keeping my distance.

"Yeah." His golden eyes were on me, not letting me go, not even for a second.

"They're coming for you," I said. "The other Guardians, I mean. They know about the warehouse."

"Good," he said.

"I told them where the hideout was." *I betrayed you*, I added silently.

"Good."

My heart started beating faster. "Sam…"

He shook his head. "Let them come, Pheebs," he murmured. "I don't care. Either they'll kill me, or I'll kill them."

I swallowed. "I'll be coming, too," I told Sam. "When the siege happens, I'll be there, fighting alongside them."

He bowed his head. "That's always been the way it's had to be, right? Why change things now?"

He was still my Sam, I realised at that moment. The months hadn't changed him. Of course, why would they? He was immortal, after all. But inside, beneath all that beauty and ugliness, he was still *my* Sam.

"My friend has turned," I carried on, steeling myself. "Stefan," I prompted. "He's one of you now."

"There are many new demons," Sam muttered with a weary sigh. "I don't bother to learn their names anymore.

There are too many to count." The snow weighed down his dark hair; he looked the same, smelled the same, moved the same. I wanted so much to be closer to him. I guess that was his charm, though. That was his power.

"Why did you come here tonight?" I asked, my voice rebounding in the quiet cemetery.

He half-smiled. "Phoebe," he murmured. "I come here every night. Just in case."

I held my breath. I didn't want Sam to sense the weakness in me. I didn't want him to know how much this was tearing me up inside. Just seeing him, hearing his voice, it brought it all back.

When would I stop? When would I finally let him go? Even when I'd thought I'd done it, even when I'd told my parents exactly where to find him, to *kill* him, I still couldn't let him go.

Stupid.

"Why did *you* come tonight?" he returned the question. "After all this time, why now?"

For you, I wanted to say. *To protect you. To tell you to run.* "A warning," I said instead, my voice cold and rigid. "Tell Leonard we're coming for him."

For a beat, Sam was silent, his expression unreadable in the moonlight. And then he laughed under his breath, a familiar desolate smile tugging at the corner of his mouth.

"Goodbye, Phoebe." He stuffed his hands into his jacket pockets and walked off into the night.

"Goodbye, Sam," I whispered. But it was too late. He was already gone.

As I watched him disappear into the shadows, I heard the screams start up again. The deafening keens wailed like a siren through the night, but they were screams for my ears only.

I dropped to the icy ground and leaned into Maura's gravestone, rocking back and forth with my hands pressed against my ears.

The Banshees were coming.

Signalling death on the horizon.

CHAPTER TWENTY-SEVEN

My dreams were full of blood, smoke and desire. Will, in his ethereal form, floated before me. His hands raised, his mouth waiting for my kiss. As I responded to his want, I felt the need to run away. But my body would not listen. My phone rang, waking me from my dream.

I rolled over in the spare-bedroom in Phoebe's home, searching for it as it blared with noise. Disorientated from sleep and burning hunger, I felt groggy and ill.

The screen showed the caller, but the number reads blocked. All I could see was Caller Unknown flashing on my screen. My thumb hovers over the accept button. Who would call this early in the morning? Was it Collette? Leonard?

I almost cancelled the call, but at the last moment, I answered. If it were a demon, I would unleash the anger that still burned within me.

I waited for the other caller to speak first. Hesitantly, as if the phone was going to attack me, I held it inches from my ear. Everything is silent, the room and the white noise of the call. Seconds dragged, and no one spoke. In the back of my mind, a flashing warning sign reminds me of something about tracking. I remembered from TV shows that people could track a location of a phone after a minute. I look at the number. I had twenty-nine seconds left.

"Stefan?" a deep voice suddenly spoke.

I didn't respond. My breathing grew heavy. The voice had an accent, one I could recall from my long-buried memory.

"Stefan, are you there?" the man asked again.

I cleared my throat. "Who is this?"

The man sounded almost sad, "I wanted this to wait until I visit, but I see I may already be too late."

"I said, who is this?"

"Stefan, it's your father."

My heart thudded in my chest.

"I'm sure you're angry right now," he went on, "but you're going to need to listen to me. I have felt your transition; your aura feels tainted with demonic residue. It means you are in more danger then you even realise. There is a lot you do not know about me. Things not even your mother would know. I had my reasons as to why I left you. I wanted to protect you from this world, but I have failed in doing so."

I was lost for words. All I could do was listen.

"I can see you are staying with other Guardians, that's good. Stay close to them. I will come to you as soon as I can."

"Is this real?" I asked although I already knew the answer. His voice I recognised, and a strange feeling swirled in my chest above my heart.

The sound of his laughter wrapped my body in warm tendrils. "We'll have time to talk about this soon. You are different, Stefan. There is still hope for you. I see your eyes; I know what it means. You are my son."

"Tell me," I muttered, a single tear rolling down my face.

"Soon…" And the line went dead.

I stared at the screen, panic coursing through me.

"No, no, no!" I shouted, hitting the glass as if it would call my father back. "Please…"

I was pleading with the dark screen, wishing for it to call again. But it stayed black.

All hope of sleep slipped away after that, leaving me more awake than before.

I flicked the switch on the side light and opened the camera application on my phone. I brought it up to my face so that I could see my reflection; I saw my new eyes.

One gold. One silver.

Half Incubus, and half… something else.

From May's reaction, I knew there was more to it.

I would find out.

Who is my father?

Who am I?

COLLETTE

Epilogue

I spat blood onto the dust covered floor.

"You have failed me," Leonard growled at me. He bent over me, hands on his strong thighs; face inches from mine. "You allowed him to escape."

I closed my eyes, trying not to think of Stef.

When I shadowed into the warehouse, Leonard was waiting for me. The moment my feet passed through the shadow my head snapped back as he hit me. Over and over Leonard beat, punched and kicked me. Stars burst behind my eyes; my body ached under his attacks. But I didn't complain. I bit down on my tongue to stifle the screams. All around me his lackeys watched on; mouths open with excitement.

He couldn't kill me. Not like this, but being immortal didn't stop the pain.

For hours I was left, sprawled across the floor until he came back for me. And the torment proceeded.

"I will not stop until you tell me if he knows," Leonard bellowed, rewinding his hand for another slap.

If keeping silent tortured Leonard nearly as much as he did to me know, I would gladly keep this up.

"I should never have picked you for this; you failed me the first time you lied."

I looked up at him through my lashes, blood dripping from cuts on my face. I took a deep breath, gathering more spit and blood in my mouth. I spat it at his feet.

"You are right, Leonard; you did fail when you picked me. I will never let you do this," I whispered from the pain.

"My mother will rise, and when she does you will be her first feast," Leonard seethed.

"Without Stefan, you will never see your mother again," I said, keeping my swollen gaze on his.

My heart sank as I said his name. Stefan. I'd tried to keep him from this. Maybe I should have killed him when I had the chance. That would have taken him from Leonard reach. But I was not strong enough.

"I will find that half-soul and use him for what I need. I can promise you that." Leonard stood tall, picking a cloth from his jacket pocket and whipping my blood from his knuckles. "I will drain that boy, and my mother will devour him. She will regain her strength and the Guardians will forever be removed from this world."

I shook my head, my hair covering my eyes. I would have swept it from my gaze, but my arms and hands were numb. I could feel the last soul I ate fixing away at my damaged body.

"You forget, Leonard; I am Stefan's sire. Without me you will never get him," I tried to stand. "But I promise you one thing. In life, I will never tell you where he is. I will never help you."

Leonard's low laughter filled the warehouse. My brother and sister demons joined in and echoed his pleasure.

I thought he was going to speak, but my vision turned back as his fist connected with my face one final time.

Printed in Great Britain
by Amazon